XCRMNTMNTN

ANDREW HILBERT

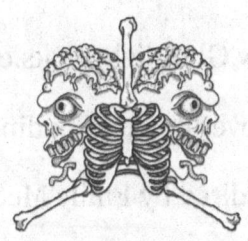

Ghoulish Books
an imprint of Perpetual Motion Machine Publishing
San Antonio, Texas

XCRMNTMNTN
Copyright © 2023 Andrew Hilbert

All Rights Reserved

ISBN: 978-1-943720-81-1

www.GhoulishBooks.com

Cover by Zug Goodina

Copy Edited by Emily McCorkle

Also by Andrew Hilbert

For Avô
For Nina

CHPTR N

INT. - KITCHEN - MORNING

MOMMY cracks eggs into a pan. She is impatient; we can tell by her spatula movements. Would it be scrambled in the end? Was she too impatient for an omelet? Would it inevitably turn flaky and nobody would like it anyways?

DADDY bites into a donut and reads the paper. Legs crossed.

                    MOMMY
          It smells like cum.

                    DADDY
     It smells like poopy cum cum.

"Oh, come on," Daddy said in between bouts of disbelieving laughter. He looked to Director. "Nobody talks like that. Who wrote this shit?"

Director was Italian. Hard I Italian. He spoke via translator. Hair greasy. Smelled of meatballs. Translator paused while Director whispered with his lips but went apeshit with his hands.

"Ah, yes." Translator nodded as Director pummeled him with air punctuation. "Everyone talks like this."

Mommy laughed. "Not in front of a baby." Mommy pointed to the cheap doll being choked by safety straps too tight in the highchair.

"Yeah, speaking of." Daddy pointed to the baby. "Nobody's going to be fooled by that Turnip Farm Munchkin. Are we going to get a real baby?"

Director was angry. He grabbed the highchair and threw it out the window.

"It smells like cum," Mommy said. But she wasn't reciting lines out of the script.

"It smells like poopy cum cum." Neither was Daddy.

If you asked anyone anywhere what Austin smelled like that day, it was so intoxicating that they'd say poopy cum cum. Some folks'd say poopy poopy cum cum. It was just that thick with fumes. Director was right. They stood at the broken window of the house they rented to film this low-budget, envirohorror near-porno. In the distance, in the middle of the great world of downtown Austin, was a pile of shit. There was no visible top. It disappeared into the clouds.

In perfect English, Director clapped his hands and said, "I know," grabbed at his heart, "I know the human spirit. Now-a, let's-a get a-back to work, no?" He clapped his hands and—swear to God—a puff of flour flew into the air.

Linguiça was the cameraman. He was a hairy son-of-a-bitch. His unibrow was as thick as his mustache. He was Portuguese, always had a bread roll in or near his mouth. "So, what? What's next?" He didn't speak Portuguese, but Portuguese-Americans absorb the culture of their people well enough without the language. They are a unique people. Some people say it's the hair.

Director grabbed a spaghetti-sauce-splattered script out of his folding lawn chair and scanned around. He pointed to a line. Translator got on his megaphone—completely unnecessary; the room was the size of a guest bathroom in a shipping container—and said, "DADDY: It smells like poopy cum cum."

```
DADDY gets out of his chair, donut
flecks sticking to the sides of his
face symbolizing his ravenous animal-
like nature, and grabs MOMMY by the
wrist.


            DADDY (CONT'D)
   The smell of poopy cum cum has
 infected my brain. I cannot control
               myself.


MOMMY's eyes widen, burning with
passion, symbolizing her ravenous
animal-like nature.


                 MOMMY
   I just want to fart and fuck until
     poop comes out of my butthole.
```

Mommy had enough. She threw the script out the window. "What the fuck are we filming here? Is this a kink film? Is this some kind of dark web nonsense? Is this even legal?"

Translator and Director stood up and circled around their folding lawn chairs.

Translator translated in real time as Director fumed in his nonsense Italian language.

"She thinks pooping is illegal? What is this woman? Is

this what they teach in America? Do they handcuff you whenever your anus loosens a little?"

"No, no, no. I do not think it is a cultural thing. I think everybody makes feces. I think maybe she's worried this is a pornography and not a cinema."

"Not a cinema? What is she thinking? Doesn't she know I am so well-known in home country that I am known simply as Director?"

"Director, yes yes yes yes yes, she knows that otherwise why would she take such a pittance to film this?"

"I saw her in the other movie, it was a titty-flick, was it not?"

"Wasn't her titties."

"Oh."

"Outside, Director, is a mountain of shit. We can re-work movie. Make something truly one of a kind and of the moment. We take a thirty-minute break. You get some meatballs and linguini, Linguiça over there can brush his back hair, Mommy can get herself together, Daddy can put his dick in some coffee, and the Turnip Farm Munchkin can get a good spitshine, and we have a whole new movie, okay?"

"Okay."

Director looked to his cast and crew—the paints he would squirt onto a blank canvas. "I do not need Translator. I a-prefer to talk in Italiano. But as-a you can see. I speak-a English with great artistry, for I am-a sculptor. From the first day of my birth, I was born in a puddle of a-spaghetti gravy. I made-a with my hands great works of art with-a potatoes and garlic and pasta. I use the a-environ-a-ment that I am dealt with. Today," Director pointed out the broken window at the mountain of poop, "God a-took a shit. We will create something new from this-a circumstance." Director looked to Linguiça. "You."

"Sim?" Linguiça spoke a little Portuguese.

"Can you make-a drone?"

Linguiça took his fur-covered, sausage -link fingers and wiped them all over his wife beater. "What are you talking about? You told me you only needed one camera. What the fuck do I look like?"

Director stopped talking again. He waved Translator over. Translator obliged the non-verbals. With Italians, it's a whole thing. Secondary sentence structure, you know, the movements of their bodies while they talk or while they don't talk. An Italian never stops talking even if they're not saying anything.

"Linguiça, please. We don't need any more of this drunken Azorean rage."

"I had one beer this morning, please." He stood up and knocked over seven to eight half-finished cans of Lone Star. The Portuguese spoke a lot with their bodies, too. But it was mostly to tell everyone around them they were drunk. Linguiça looked down at the racket of cans he made and paused for awhile, drunkenly trying to unfuck his brain while the double vision coalesced around a single vision. "I only finished one. The rest, no good. Texans can have this shit back. It's no Sagres."

Meanwhile, Mommy and Daddy sat in utter silence. They were Texans in every way. Down to their boot-shaped feet and their ass-smelling mustaches. Translator came up to them and apologized over and over again saying stuff like, "sorry," and, "sorry." But there was nothing going on in their heads. Tails tucked into their assholes at the first sign of incivility like every loud-mouthed American I've ever narrated.

It stank in there, and I suspect it stank all over Austin. Probably stunk into Kyle, Buda, Lockhart, and Round Rock too. That was a pile of shit. The base certainly covered a few blocks, and it went straight up into Heaven. Into the cosmos. Disappeared into the clouds, but you could tell it kept going.

Director was speaking in hushed tones to Translator. Translator transcribed. Translator nodded.

"Okay. Okay. Clap! Clap!" Translator did not clap physically. He said it. That's all. Cultural things. Mix-ups. "Darling, darling." Translator sat his ass down on the kitchen table and sidled right next to Mommy. "You! No more worries! No titties! We make new movie!" Director looked around the room for everyone's approval. Translator kept talking. "Daddy! You! No more getting naked. Uncomfortable, we know. No more that movie! Look outside. God gave us a gift. God gave us a chance to be something more than what we came here today as. Our state of being, our brains, our insides . . . all new now! Do you believe in God?"

Mommy and Daddy groaned, "No," at the same time. The Europeans in the room: emphatic yeses. Director looked disturbed. Translator kept on.

"How you not believe when that beautiful gift from Heaven is in Austin stinking up the everywhere?! How you not think it's a miracle?"

Daddy chewed on his prop-donut and licked the glaze off his mustache. "I don't believe in God. I don't believe in miracles. I don't believe in art. I believe in paychecks, decimal points, and zeroes."

"Look." Mommy dug in her purse for smokes. "I just don't want to be tricked into doing a movie that weird fatsos only skip around for the cumshots. If I'm going to do a movie, I want it to be good. Sex scenes are okay in my book, but I only believe in art. I don't believe in decimal points."

"I don't know why I said 'decimal points,' okay? If

you're going to linger on my one mistake, this job is going to be real tough. I thought it sounded good. I thought it matched. I already told you: I don't believe in fucking art."

Clap. Clap. Clap. Linguiça had enough.

"I throw camera in the air and we get what we got, okay? Can I borrow a cigarette? I quit, but the smell of smoke and poop reminds me of home."

Mommy gave him her cigarette. No point in giving him a full one. Freeloader. It was already lit, and half the time you let someone borrow a smoke, they dig around their pockets acting like they have a lighter and they don't. You let him take your lighter, and you never see it again. Guy who doesn't smoke ends up with a free cigarette and lighter. Unfair. Not right. No good.

"New movie. We climb to the top of that mountain. We see what is up there. This is what Director wants. New movie is two movies. One scripted. Director writes a new scene every day, constantly evolving. Movie two: documentary. Like *Apocalypse Now* and *Heart of Darkness*. Masterpiece cinema. You, Mommy, you will be good for life. Oscar winning. Daddy, you like Clint Eastwood." Translator flexed his muscles. "Hard man." Then he pointed to the doll. "Baby! You. Best Prop Oscar."

Director was at the kitchen sink scribbling and mumbling to himself. Throwing page after page of lined paper all around him. Translator jumped off the table and scurried to Director, collecting the loose paper. Linguiça was a drunk, but he was a good cameraman. He knew the moment. He started filming.

```
We zoom in slowly behind DIRECTOR. We
can see the intensity of his work as
he bobs back and forth with each
stroke of his pencil. He sweats. His
```

neck reddens. Then, just as the camera gets as close as it can without touching Director, Director looks over his shoulder, eyes fixed crazily into the camera's lens.

DIRECTOR
Take-a your naps! We start filming in-a one hours!

FADE TO BLACK AS THE THEME SONG FROM PULGASARI FADES IN

TITLE CARD:
XCRMNTMNTN

糞山

CHPTR TW

The bottom of the mountain was cold. Director and Translator were late. Mommy, Daddy, Linguiça, and Baby shivered in their summer clothes. They could see their own breaths. It's August. Very hot. Humid and stinky normally. Add a pile of shit to the city and there are problems.

"This always like this? Cold at the base of a mountain?" Linguiça's jaws clacked as he spoke. He only wore a wife beater and cut-off shorts. Huaraches, too.

"It's hardly this cold in December. I stick my finger out and I can feel the normal heat, but as soon as I get cock's-length of the mountain, I'm freezing."

"Cock's-length," Mommy stepped into the heat. "Doesn't it change?"

"If I'm aroused, which I am not, it changes." Daddy said. He was wearing gym shorts. He wasn't lying. Observably unaroused.

"From man to man, I mean."

"I'm sure you've seen your fair share." Daddy elbowed Linguiça like *Hey, we're just two dudes making a woman uncomfortable*. But Linguiça put his huarache down.

"I think this is inappropriate," Linguiça said. "And I want to make sure I state that clearly upfront and at the beginning because if I feel the need to say it again, I'll say it with my foot up your cu."

Daddy had his hands up. "Hey, hey." Chuckle. Chuckle. "I was only kidding."

"It's okay," Mommy said, shaking her head. "It really is. Thank you, Linguiça, but there's no need. I've seen a few, sure. They all look the same to me. Mostly hairy."

"Fair. That's fair." Daddy wasn't comfortable extending the conversation. Linguiça had chicken-finger toes with patchy hair. He had no desire for them to be anywhere near his ass.

In the distance, Director and Translator hobbled down the street. They were dressed for mountain weather. They had backpacks and rolling luggage things.

Yelling, hands flailing, Director makes no sense to anybody this far.

Translator dropped his things and sprinted toward the mountain. When he got to everyone, he took a few moments to catch his breath. He wheezed as snot came flying out of his nose. "You brought change of clothes and provisions, no?"

Everyone was empty-handed except Linguiça who had a plastic bag full of tall cans and beef jerky.

"No." Daddy took a step away from the mountain and to Translator. He pushed him. Just a little. But it meant business. "My contract said food would be provided and there would be no overnights and any prop food was mine, too."

"I have bad news," Translator said. "There is no more eating in the script except for the part where you fall to your knees and look to the punishing hot sun and scream and you put shit—the mountain—into your mouth."

Daddy was perturbed. You knew he was, too, because he said, "I'm perturbed by this."

Director was confused. He whispered to Translator.

"You know why no bring food?" Translator asked as he gnawed on peppered salame.

"I—you know, I don't use this word lightly—I'm fucking flabbergasted. This is the most unprofessional film shoot I've ever been on, and I shit into a cup for some art flick for two girls in college."

"It's okay, it's okay." Mommy rocked Baby. Baby was a doll. Baby wasn't fussing. But Mommy was consoling Baby. "You're making Baby cry."

"Why don't you name that hunk of Chinese plastic if you're so attached to it?" Daddy was flabbergasted, indeed.

"It's called being a fucking professional." Mommy rocked and cooed and Baby stared at Mommy with its dead, painted eyes.

Director whispered to Translator. Translator to Mommy: "Step away from the base of the mountain."

As soon as Mommy obliged, she dropped Baby.

"Mountain casts spell," Translator said. He nodded. "Baby just doll. Baby doll, see?" He grabbed Baby by the ankle and shook it upside down. Then he grabbed it with two hands and swung it like a baseball bat. Then he threw it on the ground. "No life." Now, for sure, anyways. "Director! Do we have any linguini to share?"

Director reached into a Ziploc bag in his pocket and nodded.

"We share on the mountain. You," Translator pointed to Daddy, "you eat the shit mountain in the script. We can replace with chocolate if we find any along the way."

Linguiça laughed. "Where are we going to find chocolate, cowboy?"

But Translator stepped on the foot of the mountain and checked his shoe. Full of shit. Stinky. His eyes were cloudy now, and they seemed to be further apart from each other than when he wasn't standing on the mountain. "The a-*chocolat* store."

Then, Director stepped onto the mountain. They

followed. Linguiça was last, and he filmed as they trudged upwards to stinky Heaven. Translator turned to Linguiça. "Be natural. Be awake. Be alive. Be yourself. This is the documentary part. Make sure you hear everything."

Linguiça heard everything. He heard himself as a boy in Artesia, California, throwing rocks at cars. He heard the fear somebody would stop and start shooting at him. They weren't words he was thinking, and he couldn't tell if he was thinking in words now, either. Some words, sure. But his thoughts felt like blobs leaking out of milk crates and burning onto the concrete. Then the sound of avó's house washing the thoughts away into the perfect, green grass to feed the soil to sprout new memories that weren't words or blobs or anything. Matter is no matter. It is neither created nor destroyed, merely transformed. The same matter at the beginning is the same at the end, further apart and more alone.

Is this like any other set you've worked on?
Set? I don't think this is a set.
Is it believable?
Believable? I mean look at the blood at the bottom of the mountain. That looks pretty fucking real to me. It's brown, not red; it's not like the movies. It's real.
So all those cops? They looked like real cops. Real ambulance, too.
I thought it was weird. Seemed like a bigger production than Director could afford.

Linguiça was having a hard time pulling apart who was pushing words out of their mouths. Their voices became the same. Underwater; bubbly. But he pointed his camera wherever he thought the sound was coming from.

"What are you doing?"

Linguiça pointed upwards to the sound. It was Director, Translator, Mommy, Daddy, and Baby about a futbol field's length away from him.

Director laughed, nearly fell, and rolled like a pig in shit. Linguiça could smell the tomato gravy from Director's mustache cut through the wall of fecal particles.

"You're turning around in-a circles, you clown!" Translator imitated him. He stood in place and twirled, shaking his hand wildly up and down and side to side. "Unusable footage, I'm-a sure!"

Linguiça shrugged and opened a can of Lone Star. He filmed his upward trek toward his compadres, only scanning upward when he took sips of his can.

"I can't taste nothin' up here," he said.

"It's the beer," Daddy said. "Tastes like water. Bad water."

Mommy said, "Okay."

And they both let silence linger too long because they hoped Linguiça would offer one to them.

"I mean, like my tongue feels weird."

"Open up." Mommy pried his mouth open to take a look. "Fat. Swollen. You're likely allergic to something."

"Fuck it." He gulped the rest of his can and threw it up the mountain. Gravity sent it right back against his head. But it was full. And the label had changed. It was Sagres. And as he finished reading the label and feeling how ice cold it was, it became a six pack before it became a twelve pack.

"Let's party."

Like rats, Mommy and Daddy reached into the twelve pack before Linguiça could finish his invitation.

Translator huddled with Director for a brief moment before he turned and screamed, "Chianti?!"

"Chianti?" The word bubbled out of Linguiça's mouth

as his eyes followed it and waited for the letters to pop. The word floated beyond sight.

Daddy did the thing he did when he felt superior to somebody. He smirked at Mommy before looking directly into Linguiça's drunk eyes and saying, "It's a kind of wine from the chee-anti région of Italy."

Translator laughed. The sound reverberated in Daddy's skull like somebody was putting their hand on the back of his head and pushing him further and further down the water. He would have to breathe again sometime, but there was no air for him, and he was panicking.

A loud burst like a million cannons firing at once from above, punctuated with unearthly shades of everything, stopped Daddy from suffocating. Chianti bottles rained from the sky. Director smiled. They weren't even a horse's dick length up from the foot of the mountain.

"Time is different." Mommy looked at her wrist. "No wristwatch. Nobody wears them anymore. Even the people that do wear them don't wear them there."

"Why are you narrating your thoughts?" Linguiça stuck his camera all the way against her forehead. He could see nothing, but he was trying to break through the flesh.

"Did you hear my thoughts?"

"I was listening, yes."

"Did I say them?" Mommy pushed away at Linguiça's chest ,but he was immovable. Linguiça pushed the lens harder into her forehead.

"There is nothing but darkness."

Translator pried the camera away from Mommy's forehead and stood between her and Linguiça. "While you were busy making cheap, uh, art pornography nobody wants to watch, Director was writing with the fervor of a million nuclear bombs dropping upon the planet with a sensuality unseen since Ingrid Bergman laid upon the lens a half smile of seduction." He threw the scribbled papers into the air ,and they floated to their intended recipients. "This is how we film. We film with the rawness of our bloodied flesh and the structure of our bones. We are human, yes?"

"Yes," trancelike, they answered in unison.

Director's greasy mustache combed itself into pizza-box Italian curls. He was pleased. He nodded.

                    MOMMY
   I should have worn better shoes if
   only I had known we were making the
      trek to an as-of-yet undiscovered
   mountain in the middle of the city.

                    DADDY
      It's not every day one appears.

                    MOMMY
   I wonder how many people are dead.

                    DADDY
      (angry, animal eyes, sweaty)
   We're alive. We're alive, and that's
            all that matters.

   We pan to BABY wriggling on the
   floor, covered in mud.

                    MOMMY
            I dropped him.

                    DADDY
      He will be the start of a new
                society.

```
                    MOMMY
              How did I drop him?

                    DADDY
     He will be the foundation my church
               is built upon.

                    MOMMY
              I forgot about him.

                    DADDY
       Shut up. He will be a fair king.

                    MOMMY
           I didn't know I dropped him.
```

"CUT!" Translator walked away from Director, who had his hands clasped at his mouth as he watched the words he had just written spill out into the world. He nodded his head and closed his eyes. Translator clapped. "That was beautiful."

"I don't understand it." Daddy looked at his paper. "What are we filming?"

"I dropped him." Mommy was on her knees next to Baby. To everyone else, Baby was a plastic piece of crap made in China. But Mommy still saw Baby in the script. Wriggling in the muck, crying, screaming, red-faced. Baby smelled like plastic lavender; the kind of scent chemically bonded to make toys smell less like cancer and more like good-smelling cancer. "I forgot he was here."

"We all forgot," said Daddy. "He's a fucking toy."

Mommy heard this, and her tears stopped. She got up perfectly straight and walked away from Baby, still covered in shit on Excrement Mountain.

CHPTR THR

The rest of the day they meandered. They took in the sights. They hadn't made much progress up the mountain. They still could not see its peak. But the earth below them looked different. Outside the mountain, the city looked blue-and-red tinted like an old 3D movie. Inside the confines of their new box, the colors were saturated and supernatural. Daddy noted that he felt like he could see new colors. Like his eyes had grown new cones to see the colors insects could see. "It's overwhelming," he would say occasionally to himself. Nobody heard him because nobody was listening to any externalities. Their brains were popping with new stimuli to absorb and untangle. "My brain feels croissant-shaped," Linguiça muttered. How he could feel the inside of his brain is anyone's guess, but I tell you, he could. "Buttery." Mommy clutched Baby close to her chest to keep it warm from a bitter cold only she felt. She could smell every atom of the plastic Baby was shaped from.

"What exactly are we doing here?" she asked Director. Director looked to the sky and spoke what sounded like Italian, but she did not speak Italian. She could hear the sounds, and her brain could separate them into words, but the words were absolutely meaningless. Cannoli, pizza, meat-a balls. That's all she could take out. What the fuck was he going on about?

Translator, hearing Director speak unfiltered, stopped his prayer to this holy mountain and came to translate.

"What we are doing here, yes? That is the question. We are making a metaphorical snack, like cannoli. It is sweet on the surface but, in absence of real food like uh, the pizza and meatballs, the cannoli provides sustenance. Enough sustenance to keep trudging on into the end of an existence that seems blank and silly. You, uh, see-a the top? No. Nobody sees the end. We keep going. We stuff ourselves full of cannoli, intoxicated by the sugars, and we keep going. We are going to get to the top, and when we do, we will look down as God looks down upon his creation. And then we will tumble all the way down like Jesus Christ, only to be spat on by the paupers we have given meaning to."

They stood. Empty-headed and silent. There was nothing more to ask after a speech like that. It was clear, they were working for a total fucking clo—

"Genius!" Daddy, easy to confuse and persuade, bowed at the feet of Director. He dug his face into the shit that made up the soil of the mountain. "I will follow you to the gates of Hell."

"Hell is that-a way." Translator pointed down.

Director said nothing but smirked. Daddy still had his face buried in the poop. Director tucked his foot under Daddy's forehead and lifted it out of the muck. Something came over Daddy. The way the sun shone behind Director's head like a halo. The intoxicating colors of the sky. The burning scent of the universe: poopy poopy cum cum. He couldn't help himself. Director looked like a perfect man, a perfect being. Emotion overcame him. Daddy cried.

Mommy and Linguiça gawked upon them, confused. They didn't see this overweight pizza-box-Italian as a living god.

"So what movies have you done before?" Mommy asked Linguiça.

"Movies you wouldn't watch."

"Try me."

"*Wet Cannoli* is the loose English translation. Somebody uploaded it to the internet a few years ago. Didn't matter though. Director made all his money from the backers."

"Who backed him?"

"People. I don't know. Why you asking me? The pay is decent, and I always get to have a six pack of Sagres handy."

"Where'd it get uploaded to?"

"Some porno site. I dunno. I don't partake in the sins of the flesh anymore. Mãe caught me once, and now I never do it again."

"How old are you?"

"36."

Loud organ music filled the air. One haunting chord playing over and over again in a syncopated rhythm with plenty of delay, reverb, and looping to make it disorienting. It was low, evil. And it got louder and louder until everyone's brain felt like it was leaking out of their ears. They were completely devoid of thought. Externalities and internalities melded into one and disappeared into a blank void.

The organ loops began dropping out, one row by one row. It faded into nothingness as everyone's senses recovered. The world rebuilt itself around them. There was grass, perfectly green and serene, on the shit mountain. Trees, too. They were suddenly much further up than before the organ-music void collapsed reality within them. Flute music, blue birds, waterfalls. Lavender and elderberry or some shit. Daddy was still. He looked up at Director's face. Daddy: tears streamed, snot and spit flowing from the holes on his face. He struggled to speak.

He could not. Only nonsense sounds. Only grunting. Director was pleased, but he snapped his fingers and it was over. He waved to Translator. Translator obeyed. Director's mouth to his ear. Wild hand motions. Translator nodded for every syllable. Uh-huh uh-huh uh-huh uh-huh. Yep. Okay. Translator pulled out a pen and a long scroll from his pocket and transcribed. Daddy got up and tried to catch his breath between sobs.

"Are you okay?" Mommy asked.

"I don't know. But I've felt something I've never felt before. And I am too stupid to articulate depth without somebody writing it for me, so I will do the best I can. I feel like I was in the presence of God, and he fucked me in every fucking hole I have and drained me of my own ego and my own blood, and now I am a part of the God-being forever. I am an eyeless wonder fueled by divine orgasm, and God's dick tore me into a million pieces before I fell back into his vagina. God is an orgy."

"Okay." Mommy backed away slowly.

"Do I smell like cum?"

"No."

"Okay." Daddy walked ahead of them up the hill towards the sound of the flute. He was bow-legged, his ears bled, his nose and his eyes plugged with snot and blood, and his mouth was stretched out like the elastic on basketball shorts purchased four waist sizes long ago by a fatso. His lips were chapped and dried like the ridges of an unwashed asshole.

"Maybe God did fuck him, eh?" Linguiça offered Mommy a beer.

She declined. "I'm breastfeeding." She was. The lifeless plastic doll was at her nipple but not latching. "He's having a hard time connecting to me. I don't know what to do." She expressed more milk onto the doll's face.

"He might choke," Linguiça pointed at his own nose. "Too much milk in the nose killed my twin brother."

Translator: "Let's go! Let's-a hurry, yes?! New script pages!"

"Looks good, looks brilliant, looks great. Let's go!" Daddy clapped with his portion of the scroll in his hands. He was happy. You could tell by the emptiness in his eyes.

Mommy was confused. "What are these symbols?"

Translator: "Just read it, okay?"

> MOMMY (CONT'D)
> Þ stars alight our paÞs.

> DADDY
> How is Þ child?

> MOMMY
> Þ child sleeps peacefully, abundantly
> Þroughout our journey.

> We pan to doll, eyes closed, sleeping
> peacefully and abundantly.

> DADDY
> Þat makes me happy. Look!

> Daddy points to the stars.

> DADDY (CONT'D)
> Þ lodestar alights our ways.

> MOMMY
> Praises.

```
Mommy drops child. Falls to her knees.
Screams wiÞ blood flying out of her
mouÞ.
```

Linguiça stopped filming. "Holy shit, she's really bleeding out of her mouth."

"Eyes, too." Translator looked to Director for approval, but none came. Director watched Mommy bleed with an intensity and then waved his hands in the air with no pattern, no linguistic panache; he waved his hands to the empty air like a stroke victim. Translator rushed to his side, pulled his ear down to whisper. Director snapped out of it.

"The symbol upon which you lay your eyes is the thorn. Director is looking for ways to make communication more succinct. Clearer with less confusion. The advent of putting a *t* and an *h* together to make the 'th' sound was a French perversion of the purity of the English language. The English were brutes and their language was closer to the animalism from which they evolved. The French were over-educated narcissists, intent on ruining all language with their convoluted spellings. I will bring back the thorn in my writings. I am deeply sorry that I did not explain to you beforehand." Translator clasped his hands together and smiled when he was finished.

"What the fuck were you translating?" Linguiça asked.

"Director's hand movements."

"You got all that from hand movements?"

"Yes."

"Our God is brilliant," Daddy said.

Still bleeding out of her mouth, "I kebt bronounshing ip as p."

"That's because you are not smart." Daddy said.

"You pronounced it as a d," Linguiça said and laughed as he took a bottlecap of Sagres off with his teeth.

"The d and the th are much closer lingually than the p is," Daddy said. But he was unsure. He was not a linguist. Up until now, he was a low-rate big dick for pornography nobody would ever search for. "Should we do another take?"

Director shook his head. Translator translated, "Everything is more raw the first time. Everything is more real the first time. The further we get away from acting and from factual-based thinking, the closer we get to truth."

"Okay." Linguiça was the first to start trudging upwards again. He looked down the mountain, searching for a landmark to anchor him back to Earth, but they were too high. Time meant nothing and neither did space. There was no landmark to latch onto. The view was a satellite image. They were not yet at the "pale blue dot" level of space nor were they in any state of mind to have any epiphany about the melancholy and insignificance of the universe. To Linguiça, this was still a decent gig. "I'll film some documentary footage walking backwards now." He put his eye to the camera and the world looked empty. Everyone was a floating head, bobbing softly on an empty plane. But when he looked out from behind his camera, the mountain was a paradise; serene and peaceful. He could hear birds chirp, and he saw, very clearly, everyone had bodies. Daddy crawled behind Director and kissed the ground after every step Director took. Mommy still bled from her mouth but seemed unaware as she smiled at Baby's failure to suckle. Translator walked at Director's side and chirped into his ear without any pauses. Director nodded slightly at regular intervals. Linguiça decided that the blood was going to be good for the documentary, so he zoomed in, but it did not show up when he looked into the camera. He had to guess. But guessing is tough. We are a visual species. A free-floating head on an empty plane that does not bleed is not good for the movies. So he guessed with his hands and looked over the camera. The blood was flowing out of her mouth and over her body and onto the ground and instead of flowing downward with gravity, it flowed on a path up the mountain. It flowed up and past Linguiça. Linguiça followed it. It flowed up a rock, under a tree, on a small cliff in the mountainside. It pooled into the shape of a man, and as the crew got closer, his shape became more defined.

He was nothing but eyeballs, a mouth, and blood vessels. His body was pulsating with the blood pumping fast enough to retain its shape.

"ブラッドマンです," he said.

"はじめまして," Translator answered. "トランスレーターです." Then he turned to the crew. "He said his name was Bloodman. I said *Nice to meet you* and told him my name was Translator."

"Ah, I thought that was Chinese," Daddy said. But Director smacked him on the back of his head.

Translator said, "日本語です."

"It's Japanese, you idiot." Linguiça took another swig of Sagres. "Don't you watch anime?"

Translator turned to ブラッドマン and said, "英語を話せますか."

"Of course I speak English. I speak all earthly tongues. Tongues past, present, and into the unknown ahead. I prefer 日本語, but I will speak in your preferred tongues. Each of you will hear me the way you want me to sound. To one I may sound dainty and weak while another cowers at my utterances." Daddy was bowing to Director, eyes all the way into the mud, in a puddle of his own urine—trembling at the sight of a new god. "I am all things at once, and I am nothing. I am ブラッドマン."

Director and Translator huddled. Translator said, "ブラッドマンさん, do you rot?"

ブラッドマン pondered. The silence became physical. Grains of dried blood fell out of his blood vessel ears. The rest of the bloodbody hardened and turned sandy and completely disintegrated into a pile with his eyeballs and teeth still intact atop the rubble. His eyes darted around, and his mouth clattered. He said nothing because his tongue was a pile of sand, but everyone understood because he spoke all languages to everyone in whatever one they wanted to hear him in. "Pour some water on me," ブラッドマン said.

They had no water.

Linguiça would not pour beer despite the divine freefills. "Beer is beer. Costs money down there." He pointed to the black hole where Earth was once visible.

Mommy had squirted all her breast milk onto an ungrateful plastic doll's face. Director was willing to give nothing. Director was impressed with ブラッドマン but was overall threatened by him, too. He had loyal apostles now. Translator was always at his side, but Daddy was now at his feet. Ah, yes. Daddy. He looked down on him. Director grunted and waved his hands and Translator said, "Get up, you scum. You have not-a urinated once. You have not let loose your pants to expel the wastewater of your life force from your body. When I-a have filmed *Wet Cannoli* and *The Loading Dock*, my star he pissed fifteen times a day. He tells me, he looks to me, and he tells me—lady spinning around on his cannoli—and he can't even-a pay attention. Jackhammering, and he looks at me with his-a mustache wet and greasy with poop and sweat and pubes and he says, 'Hey, Director! I gotta pee! And my scene a-no call for it!' I rolls my eyes because it's the fifth time this one day! I think to myself, I should've-a gotten into the pee-pee fetish. I have with me the Mel Gibson of piss pornography. Of course, I-a give him a break. Go pee-pee

25

in the toilet. I tell him. He does. He has to lift one of his legs behind him to balance and get the right center of gravity with the leaning tower of Pisa he has going on down there. Then he-a goes back and there is new life to the shoot. Even me, unaffected by-a the carnal pleasures. Even me, I start-a thinking I can stroke at my own creation. Like looking into a mirror. Like staring at the most beautiful man you've ever seen, lost in his eyes, you see his-a mustache and his unibrow and you think, 'ah that is a genius' and then you realize you are looking at God and you step back and it is the mirror you hung on the ceiling. It's-a beautiful. So here's what I say, go pee-pee on that pile of dry blood and see what he has to say. Write that down." Translator cleared his throat.

"Director said all that?" Mommy was incredulous. But she was trying to latch a baby doll to her nipple.

"Yes, of course." Translator scribbled something down and passed it to Director, but Director did not look at it. He put it in his back pocket.

"I don't have to pee," Daddy said.

"You have to pee," Translator said. "Director said you have to pee. I said it to you which he has said through me."

Linguiça rolled his eyes. "They start talking Bible, always." He bit into his piece of bread and pointed the camera at them.

"You need to hydrate me, or I will be scattered into the wind, and I will become nothing again." ブラッドマン was still a pile of dried blood sand with two eyeballs and a chatterbox mouth.

"I can't look at these eyes anymore," Mommy pulled out some sunglasses and put them over ブラッドマン's eyes. "It's like looking at a hangover."

Director looked at the note. He nodded. Translator got out a mason jar from God's knows where and took a scoop of dried blood to store. "It-a will make good seasoning for my meat-a-balls. And when I say mine, I mean Director's, just to be clear."

ブラッドマン screamed, "My nose!" but his pain did not last long. Daddy was unzipped and peeing. "Thank you," said ブラッドマン, and the little pile of dust pumped with life again, and ブラッドマン took shape with everything pretty much intact except for the fact that his nose was fully fleshed out while the rest of his body was still just a tangle of blood vessels. "I don't like the look."

"Where the fuck are we?" Mommy asked.

"Nowhere. You are here." ブラッドマン pointed to where his heart would be. "Always with me. We are friends now."

Mommy lifted Baby to show ブラッドマン. "Can you make him eat?"

"I can do all things for those who believe."

"Make him eat so he has life. I don't want to forget him ever again."

"Has he not been in your heart? You forget those on your brain, but you never forget those in your heart."

"Can you give him life, so he will eat?"

"I will give him more." ブラッドマン stood up for dramatic effect. "I will give him me." ブラッドマン whooshed into Baby's tiny plastic nostril holes.

Baby's plastic eyes blinked.

27

CHPTR FR

Sullen & tired, MOMMY clasps BABY to her chest and kisses over and over again. BABY is still very plastic but more responsive to her love Þan it had been ever before.

MOMMY (CONT'D)
I do not know if I can continue.

DADDY
Nonsense. We started Þis journey up Þ mountain & we will finish it.

MOMMY
What is Þ journey's point anymore? We have a child. Þ child must be protected.

DADDY
Whatever is atop Þat mountain, we will summit it & we will find out & it will give us riches we could never imagine.

> MOMMY
> God sits atop Þat mountain.

> DADDY
> Þen we will kill him, her, Þem, Þat,
> it.

DADDY looks up & sniffs his fingers.

> DADDY (CONT'D)
> We've been at Þis so long Þat my
> hands stink.

> MOMMY
> It's not someÞing I'm concerned wiÞ.

MOMMY clutches BABY tighter. BABY
squeals.

There was no squeal, though. The lifeblood given to Baby
had not endowed it with vocal chords. No crying yet.
Silence.

"What shall we do, Director? The child ruins the
performance." Daddy, a pathetic supplication.

Translator looked to him. "What is it that you want
from Director?"

"Enlightenment."

"Are you familiar with his prior work?"

"No, but I will be when we finish, and I have chance to
get home to study."

"You won't find it any longer. It doesn't exist in the way
you want it to exist."

Baby stirred in Mommy's arms. No sound, but he

jerked around violently like he could not breathe. Mommy was unaware. She stared at the stars, puffing in and out of existence. On the ground, in the city, you couldn't see stars twinkle like this anymore. The night sky from the ground was polluted gray. Here the sky was perfectly black, pockmarked with other worlds shining in and out of existence. Linguiça, dutiful with the camera against his eye, pried Baby away from Mommy's breast. Baby was blue. Voiceless. Director passed a note to Translator.

Translator cleared his throat and read it. "Dear Baby, I can't hear you, but I know you are screaming." Translator crumpled the note up and threw it on the floor. It became poop. As did everything else. The lush greenery where ブラッドマン once regaled them with beautiful moronocisms had gone to shit. Everything was shit around them again. The smell had physical stinklines emanating from all around. The landscape was barren except for the corns and pieces of spinach here and there where the ground was more fibrous—shat by a health-conscious cosmic eater. The starlight reflected off the puddles of urine that dotted the mountainside and was oddly inspiring like the crucifix submerged in piss. Cum rocks and kidney stones. Blood dots and discharge. The sights and smells were backed by arrhythmic farting and wet flapping sounds.

Daddy lifted his face from the ground and screamed at Director's feet. Director paid no attention. He was on a mission to get to the end like any good Italian who had just been given the complete *Sopranos* on Blu-Ray. Translator grabbed Daddy at an armpit and motioned for Mommy to grab from the other. Mommy, stupid from stargazing, lilted their way. She did as commanded. Daddy stank. They all stank. But Daddy stank the worst. "Why does Director not recognize me? Why does he not deign a faint gaze from upon the Mind Throne he sits?"

Translator: "If you ever want to work again after this, you will shut the fuck up. You have a-no talents. You are nothing. You are just a big dick who thinks he can play Hamlet."

Mommy: "Are you translating? Or is this you speaking?"

"Director and I are of one mind." Translator pulled scraps of paper out of his back pocket. Fleckles of shit dotted them. "Linguiça, this is for the film." And to Mommy he said, "You carry him on your back."

Þy trudg upwards. Mommy carrys Daddy on hr back. Daddy is sobbing.

MOMMY (CONT'D)
Gt ahold of yourslf.

DADDY
I'v bn forsakn by Þ gratst Þinkr of our tym.

Mommy threw her script on the ground. "I can't read this shit. What the fuck is going on?"

"I think it is perfect, Director. Absolutely perfect," Daddy said, shit all over his lips.

Director nodded at Translator as if to say, "Go off, son."

Translator paced for a moment. He walked in small circles around each person and said nothing. Silence is geographical. You can feel its distance as the words fail to leave someone's mouth. They communicate with their silence. The seconds crawl and the distance between speaker and listener grows. Listener becomes discombobulated: the desire for speech is great. The lust for another person's thoughts is insatiable, and the valley between two minds is ultimately uncrossable if not undiscoverable. Speech or no speech. Two minds cannot communicate with perfection. Translator knew this and, as a man of many languages, he wanted to make sure his patchwork thoughts quilted.

"You have been told all your lives that there is effective communication between people if only you learn the rules, yes? Is that so?" Translator's words burned like the fire of a Sunday morning sermon damning you to Hell. You fucking idiots, he told them. You fucking neanderthals. You think words can save you? The first question, the first sentence, a volley against their inner reality. "You fucking idiots, I tell you. You fucking neanderthals. You think words can save you?"

"Where's Baby?" Mommy barely listened to the intellectual dingleberries falling out of Translator's assmouth. She turned to Linguiça. His camera and his eye socket had fused together. His skin leathered over the eyepiece with pulsating tendrils of flesh, layering over one another. It was slow and sticky looking. It was a wet teratoma growth subsuming the camera. They became one.

"I can't talk now, bitch," Linguiça said. He had one hand on a cold beer and a loaf of bread occupied the other. He took a bite. "I'm trying to work. This is good shit right here."

"Where's Baby?"

But Linguiça wasn't listening anymore. Baby was at his feet, by the way. But nobody gave a shit about a doll. Only Mommy. And Mommy was distraught. Inside her head, *mommy mommy mommy where are you mommy mommy* banged against her skull. She felt tumors grow on her brain and, like lanced boils, they popped and coated her brain in more confusion. She was a kid when she hid in the middle of the K-Mart circular clothes racks. Mommy thought her mommy was coming back for her. Mommy thought her mommy was playing with her. But mommy was not playing. Mommy was going to the parking lot and not coming back. "Where's Baby?" Mommy said again. "Where's fucking Baby?!" Snot out of her nose, eyes swollen from crying. How long had she been crying for? How long had Translator paused his speech for her? She could not breathe no matter how much her chest heaved. "Where's Baby?" She couldn't get out the words. She fell to her knees, in the shit like Daddy. And there was Baby. Its painted-on neutral mouth expression now smiled in relief that Mommy was here. Mommy wasn't in the parking lot. Mommy wasn't leaving, and Mommy wasn't coming back. "There's Baby." She hugged Baby as hard as she could. "Don't you ever let me drop you again." Kiss, kiss. Kiss, kiss. "Daddy! Give me your belt!"

Daddy got up and handed over his belt. His pants fell the instant he gave it up. But he attempted to walk away anyway. He was too embarrassed to bend over and reveal to everyone how much he struggled with his weight and his perception of the struggle he has every morning dressing from the bottom up. He tripped. His face slammed right back into the shit. He could taste it. But it was better than having an asthma attack bending over.

"That's the biggest dick I've ever seen," Linguiça said. "I've been doing this awhile. Ay, Jesua."

"Another mind is unbreachable. The fortress of words can never penetrate or translate thought. Listen to the cacophony of screaming in your own minds. Words simply translate thoughts. Something is always missing. A dog or a pig experiences the same complexities we do, but their tongues are laden by God with weight to make pronouncing anything impossible. This is the truth. Director seeks to kill all which makes communication unclear. We have successfully slain the *th*. We have made the inferential jump to assuming that the thorn on its own means *the*. Now we will kill the written *e*. It is assumed. We do not need it. In fact, the more vowels we kill, the better off we are. Vowels are mind control. Some languages do not have vowels. In some languages, the vowels are implied. The reader is trusted to fill in the blanks. English is a written language that enslaves the mind by telling us everything we need to know about a singular word. More complex languages have higher literacy rates than English-speaking countries. Why is that?"

"It's probably because—" Daddy lifted his head out of the shit just to get it shoved right back in by Translator's foot.

"It's because nothing. We spoke to Bloodman. Bloodman is living Google Translate. His Japanese sucks. But his Japanese is still impressive enough to see the limitations of the English language and why it is constraining this entire production. Don't you feel it?" Translator was nearly out of breath. Director passed him another note. "It's-a like-a cold meatball with-a no spicy and a-no fettuccine alfredo sauce. Mama mia. It's a-tragedy." Translator stuffed the note in his pocket and held his hands up in the air. "Before words, were hands. We spoke with our hands. Italians still do. We want something: we point. We want to beat somebody up: we pummel. We want to call someone a jack-off: we jack off. Hands are where we're headed. Eliminate the vowels."

Linguiça was nodding. His face had enveloped the entire camera save for the lens. "I'm kinda hurting," he said. He nodded to keep his balance. The camera was heavy, and his eye socket was not as strong as his unibrow would suggest. "I'm kinda hurting real bad, man."

CHPTR FV

The greenery was over. This pile of shit was a real pile of shit. Everyone was feeling it except for Director and Translator. Admittedly, they made up two-fifths of the team, but everyone not in charge was feeling beaten. Even the Good Disciple Daddy felt the stress of staying in Director's favor. His hair was falling out. All over. But mostly on his head. And sometimes, if he scratched at his head hard enough, chunks of flesh would fall out too. It could have been stress, or it could have been the mysterious mountain that dropped out of space made entirely of poop, cum, and other excretions.

Mommy was recovering from the fear of losing Baby. She made a nice spot for herself in a pile of more-dry poop. The cum showers were a surprise at first, but they got used to them. Every hour or so, cumlet drops would rain from the sky. There wasn't much to it. The cum was cum-colored. It had a cummy smell. And, though nobody liked to admit it: tasted just like human cum, too. Director called it cosmic alfredo sauce, and he opened his mouth every time there was a weather event. His mustache was now mostly dried-up cum.

Linguiça could not stop picking at the scabs that were holding his flesh-camera to his eye socket. He couldn't get over their taste. "They're good eats," he would say as he ate them. "They taste like Linguiça." Daddy once joked that

35

Linguiça could suck his own dick, and Linguiça was referring to himself in the third person, but it wasn't a very funny joke, so it wasn't recorded here. Whether or not Linguiça could perform that acrobatic feat in the past was no matter. Linguiça wouldn't be able to do it any longer. He had a very large camera connected to his face.

Director clapped his hands and made a point of inhaling with his nostrils flaring out to at least the size of a good meatball. "Ah!" It was his first verbal utterance since they started filming however long ago that was. Time stretched funky on this mountain. It could have been years ago at this point. It could have been thirty minutes. Nobody really knew, and the three people taking orders were becoming untethered from a shared reality. Daddy, his head lighter now without the hair and chunks of flesh, was able to scurry over in a bow without dragging his face through feces. "It's a beautiful day," Daddy said.

Translator was not far off. He jogged over. "Rain dogs. They lose their way after it rains. It doesn't rain here. It cums. You are all cum dogs. Look at you. Wallowing in your own confusion. Get a grip. Get over yourselves. You don't have to understand everything. Morons."

Linguiça leaned over to Mommy. The benefit of having a camera fleshed to your face was that you could always be filming without being too worried about missing something. "How much do you think Translator runs the show?"

"Oh, I don't know. I haven't had much time to think about it since Baby keeps me awake all night." Mommy smiled and pouted and then turned her gaze back to nowhere as she rocked back and forth with Baby. Bloodman was in there, but he was trapped inside a body that could not move, and could not talk, and could not do anything but fill up empty space where thoughts go to die.

"I mean, look at Director. He looks like a fucking pizza box. I never even put it all together. *Wet Cannoli* was only a paycheck after college. Answered a Craigslist ad. Filmed it in La Palma, California. Tiny nothing-town nearby Cerritos, the real powerhouse of Los Angeles County. Nice parks, nice sidewalks, a really good Best Buy. Translator was there, but they seemed to talk more. Director didn't talk much, but he did speak, and he didn't really sound all that Italian. I couldn't really place his accent, but it sounded more Texas than European. And by the end of *Wet Cannoli* nobody spoke to anybody else, and Translator started doing all the translating. It felt like this God Cop, Talk Cop act was developed on the spot. And here we are, miss. Sitting around hugging some dead-ass doll and picking scabs at my camera face on a mountain that never ends where we can't see the top or the bottom anymore and everything feels like a cosmic void. We're in God's asshole. Or we're close to it. I can't tell. Why does it keep cumming?"

Mommy said, "Hmm," but that was as far as her acknowledgement would go.

"New pages," Translator said. "Get to it. Get up. Stop thinking."

They groaned as they got up. The creaking in their bones echoed off the mountain. Bloodman was the only life they'd seen the entire trip. And now he was trapped. Daddy wanted to kill him. He was a threat. Here Director was trying to eliminate language elegantly, and Bloodman was inside Baby plotting to keep world tongues alive. Translator was a necessary evil. He needed to know languages in order to annihilate them and to destroy the convoluted mouth sounds that approximate thought. Communication makes it all the clearer that brains are impenetrable. The inside of a person is unknowable on the outside. The attempt to know reveals the ignorance. Daddy was a zealot. A real dumbass. "I cannot wait to read what Director has divined today."

"Stop speaking in spiritual terms. We are going to get up that mountain. We are going to see God. And then we are going to wrestle him down to Earth, try him for his crimes, and then shoot him in the head." Translator was serious. Nobody else believed in God. Translator made a point of drawing a cross on the ground and then spitting on it every time he saw wet enough poop on the ground.

"I hate God," he'd say, "especially of the Christian variety. What a bunch of numbskulls." To hate God was to believe in God. He was a good Christian in the end.

"Let's go, Baby." Mommy tugged at the belt she made into a leash for Baby and dragged it around.

MMM drgs Bb rnd wÞ lsh.

MMM
Cn't gt nthng dn wÞ Þs kd rnd.

MMM sbs.

DDD
W cn stp t mk   . M stmch hrts.

MMM
Bb nds slp. Bb nds mlk.   cn wt.

DDD
Y cnstntl dn Þ nds f m flsh. WhÞr t b
crnl, nl, r fcl.

XCRMNTMNTN

MMM

Þr s smÞng bggr Þn s gng n hr. Pls dnt Þnk m nt knwldgbl f yr nds. M jst ncncrnd t f prrt. Lv y.

DDD

Y r crrct. M n lngr mslf. M w.

"I thought his fucking goal was getting closer to nature through the stripping of unnecessary fluff." Daddy was angry. "I can't get through this shit. What are you asking of me, Director?" Daddy was in his face. Director smirked and walked away.

"It is closer to animals. Animals are pure. Can you think without vowels? Make the sounds in your head. This requires you to infer and contextualize. Nobody is trying to drive you crazy." Translator grabbed Daddy by the shoulders. "Come on, you're the best actor here. We need you."

"What the fuck?" Mommy dropped Baby's leash. "He's the best actor?"

"Yes. Actor. He. You. Actress. The best."

"Wow, I guess it really is true what they say about Italians," Mommy harumphed around.

"And what is that?"

"They're fucking stupid."

"Okay, that's fine. I am comfortable enough being a polyglot that I know you did not mean that."

"Who do you actually speak for? Director or yourself?" This was Daddy. He was mad and poked his finger in Translator's chest, really bullied him around. Daddy had a big dick. He could do shit like that. "Director?! Hey, Director! This little pussy is trying to steal your shine."

Director clapped his hands like an owner would to a

dog that was eating its own shit in the house. Stop! Stop! Stop! Everyone knew what clapping was all about. No words needed. They stopped, of course.

"What the fuck is going on with these scripts?" Mommy pointed to a page and shoved it in Director's face as if he didn't write the fucking thing.

```
nw mdnss sts n & nbd cld s nw whch w
Þ wnd wld blw.
```

```
MMM swngs Bb vr hr hd wldl, ys pppng
t, mkp smrd.
```

MMM
```
M gng t fnd Þ vd t Þ nd f Þ nvrs & m
        gng t pg t.
```

"I will not be swinging Baby over my head." The realization hit her slowly, the way you don't realize you're in pain until you look down and see your legs blown off. Then it hurts bad. She wasn't holding the leash anymore. And Baby wasn't anywhere near any of the places she could have left him. Somebody was messing with her, or Baby learned to walk.

"I don't think I can shoot any more today," Daddy said.

"My eye is bleeding, I don't think I can see out of it anymore."

Translator said, "Okay, fine. We rest. We get back tomorrow. Is that okay, Director?"

Director nodded.

Translator: "Just point the camera by using your good eye as a tracker. The shots will be fine."

CHPTR SX

As they slept, the universe swirled around them. Daddy slept fine. All he had to do was shut his eyes, and he was out. Linguiça's indigestion and constipation made it a fitful rest. Translator and Director were off in a cave, away from everyone else because they were the leaders. They had the vision. They needed to be apart. Mommy could not sleep. She was haunted by the constant pitter-patter that encircled their camp. It was Baby. Baby could walk, and she didn't get its first steps on film. She didn't even see it. Bad mother, terrible. Uncaring and too dedicated to her work, probably. That's what people would say. You can't win. Mommy got up and looked around. She saw nothing. It was too dark. This high up, the only light pollution was from celestial bodies, and tonight they did not shine. They were in the void again.

The tiny feet clomping against wet poop sounded squishy but faint. Baby weighed next to nothing. But Mommy had motherly senses and could hear so much as an eye opening. She crouch-walked to make herself as silent as possible. She didn't go on her tiptoes because she read that doing so was noisier. Flat-footed was the best way, especially with shoes on. March, march, march. Baby's steps were in surround sound and moved at an impossible pace.

"Baby! Baby! Where are you?"

41

The movement stopped. The sky turned blood red. She could see everything now. Piles of skulls, puddles of blood or pee or cum, screaming, gnashing of teeth. It was hot and humid, and Mommy's hair poofed up with frizz. She sweat through her shirt. Her stomach turned. She vomited. She shit herself and pissed herself and had to take off her clothes. Mommy looked for Daddy. Daddy was asleep but Linguiça was sitting upright at a perfect ninety-degree angle. He faced her with his dripping-blood-camera affixed to his face. Skin tags and warts had taken over his flesh. "I used to get them as a kid!" Linguiça assured nobody. "Now I just get them on my ass! All you gotta do is tie some thread around the base real tight. It loses blood flow, and it falls off." Underneath Linguiça was a pile of dried-up skin tags. "They've been falling off all night. I hope they don't reach my balls. It's hot."

Linguiça felt it, too. His clothes dripped with sweat and got too heavy and stuck to the prodigious chest and back hair he sported. He didn't like that feeling. He didn't like cloth against skin, especially when both were wet. He wore billowy clothing to hide the shape of his body. He always looked pregnant. "When I was married and my wife was pregnant, I'd joke I was bigger than her. I gotta get in on myself first before anyone else does. Otherwise it hurts too much. I've always been told I was too sensitive."

"You're not even that big."

"Yeah, but we Portuguese get those spherical guts. It's bad for us."

"You had a kid?" Mommy was impressed.

"Never came out. Umbilical cord got him. This was a long time ago, so I don't miss the fucker or the cow he died out of." Linguiça had to get ahead of his own emotions before anyone else could. He felt some pressure in his sinuses like he was about to cry, and that would have been

devastating for him. "Now I'm single and ready to mingle."
The joke didn't land. They never did. That wasn't the point.
The point was to halt all conversation in which he might
be the center.

"We need to find Baby."

The footsteps were loud now. It wasn't like a Cabbage
Patch Kid was running around anymore; it was like a full-
grown, plus-sized man was now running around. A fucking
elephant. The light around the mountain strobed in and
out. The blood-red tint to everything disoriented them.
Their sweat looked like blood, their naked bodies looked
like blood, and, when they were done examining their own
perplexities, they looked up to the sight of a twenty-foot-
tall Baby clomping toward them.

"赤ちゃんです。"

"Bloodman!" Linguiça screamed. "We don't speak that
language!"

"I am Akachan. I am Baby. I am the universal product.
I am mass produced. I am forgotten. Tied to a leash.
Dragged about. In a pile of shit. Bloodman needed a body,
I needed consciousness, and together we became the
beautiful specimen you see here."

"Baby! Baby! Mommy loves you!"

Baby lifted his plastic foot in the air. He could crush
Mommy. He could. She was, after all, who Bloodman
deemed The Entity Who Leashes. She would deserve it. But
she also gave him milk though he was not her child. He was
a piece of ugly plastic found on the clearance rack by an
incredibly lazy visionary Italian director named Director.
Baby's foot dangled high above Mommy. Mommy paid no
attention to her hovering death. She was so happy to see
Baby. So happy to see that Baby had grown on his own and
found a way to survive without her. That's just good
rearing.

Blood leaked from Baby's eyes. As each drop hit the ground, the blood formed into the shape of a man. Bloodman. ブラッドマン. The blood vessels formed and his eyes plopped in and his chatterbox mouth floated where they would normally be on his face. He was twenty-five feet tall too now. "Osmosis. Blood fills up all the space you give up. Plastic can warp. Miracles do happen. 赤ちゃんさん! Kill your mother!"

But 赤ちゃん was thoughtless again. Nothing animated his body anymore. He had no intelligent being to keep him balanced. The wind could knock him down and kill them all. This would be a terrible time for a cumstorm. ブラッドマン had not thought this through because the first fuffles of pre-cum had already begun to fall. Linguiça stuck his tongue out to make sure it was cum and not snow. "Definitely cum."

ブラッドマン vomited blood. It covered everyone. Linguiça could feel the blood seeping into his pores; Mommy felt like her body and ブラッドマン's body became one. They screamed as the blood entered their bodies. Director, Translator, and Daddy wandered around and followed the screaming only to be enveloped by the blood and cumstorm. Director licked his mustache over and over again in an empty attempt at keeping it clean.

"To the man who refuses to speak," ブラッドマン yelled, "I will have his tongue!" ブラッドマン lurched forward, his body in constant vibration and flow as the blood vessels that shaped it pumped toward a nonexistent heart. Daddy stepped in front of Director and absorbed ブラッドマン's blow. His bones shattered, all of the blood in his body came out of his asshole, and his skin melted into the mountain.

"There is no healing those bones." ブラッドマン's voice was inside all of their heads, heard the way each one imagined a body like his would speak. "Another's brain is unbreachable. But I have breached, I have run over the walled cities of your thoughts. You will never escape me for I am immortal." ブラッドマン grew and grew until his toe was the size of their entire bodies. "You who seek to enslave me will perish." ブラッドマン's voice produced shockwaves that blasted Baby off its feet. Baby fell on top of Daddy, splattering whatever remained of him all over everybody else.

"Let's work together!" Mommy yelled and pushed at Baby's plastic body to roll it off Daddy. Linguiça and Translator joined in. Director stood aside and gawked at ブラッドマン. It was no use. Baby was too big, and Daddy was too dead. As soon as they rid themselves of ブラッドマン, they would hold a memorial for the man they hardly knew. Mommy noticed Director did nothing to help them. "He died for you." Director said nothing. Director did not give so much as a sideways glance at Mommy. He smirked, though, and he crossed his arms— proud that Linguiça's camera was always on and always affixed to his face. This was going to be one hell of a movie.

"This is some kind of riddle," Linguiça said. "What does blood hate?"

"What?"

"What does blood hate? How do we kill blood?"

"What?"

"When I was a kid, I used to rub poop into my scabs. Everyone thought I was crazy, but I knew that blood hates poop."

In the shade of Baby's chemically fragrant body, Mommy and Translator looked at Linguiça perplexed. "Blood doesn't have thoughts," Translator answered as soon as the stench of cum, blood, and feces became more noticeable than their confused silence.

"Poop infects blood," Linguiça said, and he grabbed a handful of excrement from the ground and pelted ブラッドマン's legs. "Look at how it sizzles with pus every time I hit him. Look at the bottoms of his feet!"

As ブラッドマン stomped around, they tried to catch a glimpse of what the fuck Linguiça was going on about. "Like Hell," Translator said, "He might be onto something." The bottoms of ブラッドマン's feet were green and rotting. The blood did not flow down there. They were calloused scabs flaking away into amputation.

"Keep throwing poop."

They did. They grabbed handfuls and threw as much as they could as high as they could.

"Cut him off at the knees!"

The more shit they flung, the more ブラッドマン became infected. His blood vessels constricted and stopped flowing. They turned to rust and speckled away with the wind. Inch by inch, they cut ブラッドマン down. It took hours, but eventually he was nothing but a screaming head. Linguiça stuffed some excrement into ブラッドマン's eyes. "Pink eye is a real bitch, kid."

Mommy shoved poop into ブラッドマン's mouth. "You talk too much shit."

Translator stuffed some into ブラッドマン's ears but he couldn't think of anything appropriate to say. ブラッドマン writhed in agony. "I cannot die," he said. "Please, end your torture."

Other than covering his entire face with shit, there wasn't much they could do to kill him. They were tired, anyways. He probably learned his lesson. Director clapped. His smile could have decapitated him. It was the most emotion anyone had seen from him since they started filming.

Translator got up from their shit-flinging ditch. "This

was-a brilliant! It's-a so great to see everything working-a out! Linguiça! Did you catch it all?"

Linguiça's face was melting with infection. He was almost all skin tags, bruises, and scabs. He gave Translator and Director a thumbs up. From Director's hands emerged a glass box. Director put it on the ground. Then he pointed to the giant, dying head of ブラッドマン. Translator nodded. "The head goes in here."

Linguiça and Mommy dutifully rolled the head over to the box. ブラッドマン was lighter than he appeared. He was blood and vessels. It made sense.

"Thank you for not killing me," ブラッドマン said. "I am an indifferent force. Neither evil nor good. The rest of your short lives would have been spent wondering about my death."

Mommy's body was numb. The blood and cum from the storm had hardened into armor around her soul. Inside, she was screaming. Inside, she saw herself in a tiny box screaming and trying desperately to kill herself. But the box had nothing. It was a tiny pocket of space devoid of any mass except for her own broken heart.

"We eat Baby tonight," Translator said.

Internal pain became an external physicality. Mommy puked. Linguiça tried to hold her hair back but it was no use. He was a weakling with vomit. He threw up, too. Translator and Director were unaffected. Instead of concern, they moved to Baby and started to roll him over.

"This plastic will taste good," Translator said to Director. Director nodded. Beneath Baby, Daddy was a pile of blood and melted flesh that still, somehow, emanated consciousness.

"Help me." If a pathetic rat had a stupid voice, that's what Daddy sounded like to Director. But Director was a benevolent dictator who could empathize with his sycophants. "Director, this is the most important experience of my life."

"You will-a never walk again. You will never have any bones. You will merely be a puddle, lucky to not be swept away by a janitor in the middle of the night," Translator said. "Yet, you are conscious. You are worthy of our pity." Translator pulled out a one gallon Ziploc freezer bag, and dumped Daddy into it. "You are tiny now, but your thoughts are still large. No vessel can contain your essence." Translator spoke softly, as if to conceal his intentions from Director.

If Daddy had working tear ducts, he would have sobbed. It was the nicest thing anyone had ever said to him. Once he was just a big dick for hire, now he was tiny. No vessel could contain his essence. It was the Hallmark card moment for being stuffed into a Ziploc bag. Translator zipped it up, and Daddy looked with his deep love and admiration of Translator and wonder at the way it sounded from the inside of the bag. The air was humid with his own breath circulating and recirculating. The condensation from his breath fogged up the sides of the Ziploc, but it was the most comfortable Daddy had been in a long time. His face was no longer always in the shit; his body was no longer bowing in constant deference. Now, he was fully submitted to their love and guidance. His life was at their mercy and without any ability to act—he no longer had to worry about the consequences of his own missteps. He was angelic and sinless now; a formless puddle of human with desires and jealousies and iniquities that could never manifest outside the confines of the Ziploc bag.

Baby could not scream as Translator and Director did their best at cutting pieces of its body to eat. They were artists, not mechanics. They were visionaries, not ditch diggers. They were sensitive. Their hands were weak from pointing out tasks for others to do that they could not do—something as simple as chopping off a limb of a giant plastic Baby with no tools designed for the task. Director gave up and slunk to the ground, his back rested on the foot of Baby. He gave Translator a look. Translator began writing.

 CHPTR SVN

MMM (CONT'D)
Bb dd. W mst t. W mst chp nt pcs.

DDD
Hv n rms. Hv n lgs. Jst bg. M slss.

MMM
Ts m dt t tk cr f Þs mslf. Brght Bb
n. Nw mst cnsm hm.

MMM grbs rck. Shrpns rck fr hrs. Swt,
bld, nkd. Hrs. Rl tm.

"I can't sharpen it anymore!" Her eyes had sunken inches into her skull, surrounded by a deep blackness. She had pink eye now, too. Not an unexpected side effect of being in an atmosphere more shit than air.

Translator: "Now start cutting. Start with the toes, yes? Start with the fingers, yes? Easier to cut. But then after the hours you take nakedly screaming and dismembering Baby, you will have to cut out its heart and eat it first out of respect."

Daddy, you could barely understand him because he was in a Ziploc bag, said, "I don't think he has a heart." But nobody paid him any attention. That was the good of the bag. Translator clutched it whenever he wanted to and put it down somewhere nobody could hear him when he wanted to. Daddy had no agency. He had a voice but no say-so, so nobody listened.

True believers are ready to go from the start. Daddy was a true believer. Director was a visionary. He turned no-budget pornography into art, and that was Daddy's ticket out of the fuck scenes filmed in the walk-in refrigerator at the place he barbacked for. They called him the bareback barback. He said no to nothing and yes to everything, and he could have whatever jobs he wanted on account of his hefty dick. "You can go on forever," directors would say in excitement. There was no need for sticking anything up his ass after ejaculating to keep it going. He just kept going. It was less of a talent and more of a disability. Daddy couldn't cum. His body didn't produce cum. He had balls, sure, but what he had in the length and girth of his penis he lacked in nuts. They were tiny. Smaller than raisins and whenever he got a physical, the doctors would comment on the boba-like consistency of his tiny grapenut testicles. Daddy was always on edge. But the size of his dick made up for a lot. Nobody ever balked when he said, "I don't do cumshots." Some college intern could add cum in post.

When he signed up for Director's new project, he was hopeful. The casting call said very clearly in bold font: **THIS IS NOT A PORNOGRAPHY. THIS IS AN ART PROJECT FROM FAMED ITALIAN DIRECTOR: DIRECTOR.** Anyone whose name was Director was born to do this shit. Daddy'd never heard of him. And he was too strapped for cash to do any research on the project. Now he was here. In a Ziploc bag. A formless mixture of Hope in service to Art. In service to making people proud of him. This thirty-something, sterile fuck machine would amount to more than mopping up throw up. He would serve truth through art. He would suffer though he didn't understand the point.

"And that is the point," Translator said. "There is no need to understand anything. People are obsessed with nice endings that tie everything together. They are obsessed with development, continuity, understandability, logic, rationality. It's all nonsense. Have any of these complainers lived in the real world? Car crash! Boom! You die. Plague, masks, coughing, dying, denial, recovery. War over dirt piles. A pile of shit falls in the middle of Austin, and the people of the city go on about their day on their little scooters. How many dead bodies are under us right now?"

Daddy couldn't help but feel his thoughts were being listened to. How did Translator make such a perfect transition from the inner thoughts of Daddy's mind. Well, he couldn't see too much outside the bag, but he could make out that the sky was filled with green text, constantly updating. Face west: Mommy. Face east: Daddy. Face north: Baby. Face south: ブラッドマン. Look up, and it was Director's thoughts. Devoid of vowels. Devoid of consistency. Completely barren of useless thoughts. Every thought from Director was a golden slice of truth. Manna from heaven. Translator's thoughts did not appear. The world revolved around their journey. Daddy was committed to seeing it to its conclusion.

Mommy straddled Baby's foot and jammed the rock against its pinky toe. Nothing happened. No dents, no scratches; just a tingling feeling in her funny bone. "It's hard as hell!"

"It's no use," ブラッドマン said. "There is no meat inside. There is no blood. I gave 赤ちゃん life. Before me, 赤ちゃん was a cheap prop. After me, 赤ちゃん will continue to be a cheap prop. There is no life in there."

Director had his hands out, shaped like a widescreen, to frame this failed scene. He motioned to Linguiça to move to where Director stood and shoot from there. Linguiça lumbered over, his body turning blue, and more and more blood was needed to power the camera. By now, gravity pulled the weight of the camera downwards and caused Linguiça's flesh to tear. "We gotta tripod?" Linguiça looked around.

Director shook his head. Linguiça grabbed the box ブラッドマン's head was in, sat down next to it, and propped the camera over the top. The blood from where his face was tearing off pooled beneath the camera. ブラッドマン's mouth got big with excitement. He chomped at the blood that he could see but could not touch. Translator kicked the box. "Shut the fuck up." Just like Translator did to his dog when she showed any signs of innocent hunger. Translator turned to Mommy: "Okay, scream."

Mommy screamed. Her ears popped from the screaming. With her eyes closed, she felt like she could see the colors of her rage and confusion. Flashing white, blood red, the weird peachy color of Baby's plastic skin. This fucking mountain. The pointlessness of it all. She would be nothing more than the actress who thought she wasn't doing a porno until shoot day. This was the way out. This was going to be high falutin' Oscar bait. This was *Apocalypse Now* and the documentary *Heart of Darkness*. This was the new frontline of cinema in a world where everything had already been done and had already been done better. They were going to be high-minded and worse on purpose. She was intoxicated by the brilliance of the pitch. In big words on the casting call: **THIS IS NOT A PORNOGRAPHY.** It was perfect. Rule-breaking. Envelope-pushing (for her). She opened her eyes and stopped screaming. She couldn't scream anymore anyways. Her vocal chords were shot. Her ears bled. She looked around at everyone, just as tired as she was. Even Translator showed signs of wear. Director was the only one blissfully unaffected.

Then, he spoke for the first time since the pile of shit landed. He clapped his hands and said, "Okay, let's go," in a very American-sounding tone. There was no hint of marinara on that tongue. It was all hot dogs and cheeseburgers. Complete silence fell on them. All the screens displaying their thoughts went blank except for Director's. They looked upwards to the heavens and read his brain.

"Oh, fuck," it said.

CHPTR GHT

"**I've never even** been to Italy," Director admitted. "But you don't get people to fuck on camera by telling them that you work at Subway and still live with your great grandma in your hometown."

"Within lies lies the truth." Translator nodded.

"Thank you, Translator." Director put his hand on Translator's shoulder. Translator grasped it, tears streamed down his face.

"I'm so tired." Translator looked around at the blood-soaked, naked bodies in front of him: Linguiça with this camera breaking his face; Daddy, a puddle in a Ziploc bag; Mommy riding the foot of a giant plastic baby doll she had convinced herself was her own. ブラッドマン who was some demon they came upon on their journey. He would elicit no sympathy from them. He tried again.

"I do not want you to feel like I've lied to you this entire time," Director said. "All of my ideas are real. Translator helps me in all things. He translates my own mind. We have a bond. I am at war with written language. I am at war with all that weighs down the human mind. My caricature of an Italian auteur was a living commentary on your own expectations."

"Oh, shut the fuck up, you sack of shit." Daddy, all dirty with shit and in a plastic sack, spoke up. "You're an overeducated, under-talented narcissist. Just like every creator. Just like God Himself."

"Theirself," Translator said.

"Themselves," Director said.

Black thunder struck the top of the mountain, a sight they had never seen up until this moment. If you can see it, you can take it. It was almost done. They were in space now. They were outside the grasp of Earth's selfish embrace. They looked down at that pale blue dot and laughed. If only the fuckers down there could experience whatever the hell was going on right here. Then they'd know something about life. What, exactly, nobody knows.

"I like him more knowing he's a fucking fraud," Mommy told Linguiça. Linguiça didn't acknowledge anything anyone said. Death had begun for him already. But they all marched upwards towards the top. Upwards to meet God.

"Wait." Director stopped leading. "We need to have my funeral." Here he was not dying, and this motherfucker wanted to have a funeral for himself. "We must kill the old way if we are to continue." It was all about him. Of course. "Linguiça!" He snap, snap, snapped. "You're rolling?"

"I'm . . . always . . . rolling." His face and camera were slumped forward, staring at the ground.

"Film something other than your own feet. That art period in my life is over. I appreciate the breadth of your knowledge of my output, though."

"What?" Linguiça couldn't breathe. He wheezed through even his thoughts. He had inhaled too much shit.

"Never you mind. You do what it is you are best at: listening to my orders in exchange for a wage."

"Hey! You can't talk to him that way!" Daddy screamed but nobody heard. Linguiça was too weak to be offended. "Give him a beer!"

Linguiça perked up at that. "Yeah . . . " he said. "A beer.

Like the good old days. How long have we been doing this?"

"Time up here in space doesn't work the same as it works down there on Earth," Translator said.

"Yeah, yeah, yeah," Daddy said. "I read about that. Like we're in a hologram or something." Nobody cared what he said, no matter what angle he tried: righteous indignation or nodding in agreement to the superior intellectual speaking.

"Yes, or something . . . " Translator dismissed him.

If only I could kill myself, Daddy thought.

"Tonight! We bury the old *we* and celebrate the birth of the new us!" Director pointed to the top of the mountain. "That is what we have been suffering for!"

CHPTR NN

Organ music droned. Wilted flowers were strewn about a small path toward a candlelit cave where Director rested in his coffin. It was an ornate coffin with beautiful woodwork. Angelic faces looked upward even from the clouds they sat on. The casket was open, and Director had Translator embalm him. He looked dead, and maybe, for that small period of time, he was dead. His hands were clasped together over his chest, and his face was still. If he breathed at all, they were tiny inhalations and exhalations, imperceptible to anyone. His mustache was clear of all cum and feces. He was beautiful in his slumber.

Mommy still had no clothes and was caked in blood. Linguiça, too. The funeral was for all of them, so maybe once they buried Director, they would get hosed off and made anew. Maybe not. Linguiça carried Daddy in his Ziploc bag. ブラッドマン's transparent box sat in the first row of empty chairs. Translator stepped up to the lectern.

"Good evening, friends." He cleared his throat. "We are gathered here today to dispose of the lie we believed about Director. You see, Director is uniquely dedicated to his art. While he made no-budget pornography for his friends and internet strangers, his porno still sought much more than cheap ejaculations. He imbued everything he did with meaning and sacrifice. Maybe that was his downfall.

"He didn't see life to be lived meaninglessly. He didn't

see life to be lived with no passions or goals. He built his own costume and lived every minute of every day inside his character, fooling even those closest to him. Fooling even me. I'm not proud of the part I played in his lie to you all, but I am proud of this: Director and I were a team. Now, I look at him bloated and rotting away, and I don't see wasted potential. No. I see potential that stretches further than the flesh caskets we give ourselves. We are a part of a metaphysical vision. Taking part in somebody else's vision is the highest form of creation.

"When God created Earth, he did as any creator does. He diligently labored over small details. He built a world with rules in the form of physics and mathematics. He spit into a petri dish and watched bacteria form. He took an interest in every character that emerged whether they were planned or not. And then, bored, he walked away to pursue something else.

"Watch *Wet Cannoli*. You can see the moment Director became bored with the endless flapping sounds of ballsack against asshole. You can see the disdain he had for the entire project by the credits. The cumshot and then it's over. Director was interested in the relationship built between those three men and eight women in the Italian bistro after hours. But he knew the audience was not. What came after the cumshot? Did they exchange numbers? Did they meet for dinner? Did they fall in love? Director was interested in these human questions. By the end of the hour-long shoot, Director was disinterested. He pioneered the No Fluffer Method. Out of limitation comes innovation. His films prior, to cut costs, Director would handle the fluffing himself, but thanks to a bad case of tennis elbow, Director had a lightbulb go off. *What if we cut the fluff?* You can see it in *Wet Cannoli*. It takes forever for the men to get hard on camera. It's awkward being directed by a genius, and yet, *Wet Cannoli* was the most streamed longform pornography that summer. It's because Director took time to explore on camera what made a man hard.

"Nobody expects an award for the very necessary drudgery that is making erotic film. Sure, the industry has its own circle jerk every year, but Director didn't care about the adoration of a select few. Director cared about the education of the masses. He felt the best way to teach deep truths about human nature was to make even the fleeting moments of arousal a class on philosophy. Countless men and women, in their own homes, spent twenty minutes of shame searching for something to release themselves to. It didn't need to be completely mindless Onanism. It could be deeply intellectual. That is what Director strove for.

"It's true, this—" Translator motioned around him, "—this all started off as a low budget porno. But Heaven and God gave us a gift. *Poopy Poopy Cum Cum* was going to be a scat film, and what do you know? A pile of shit dropped into the middle of the city, killing a countless many, so that we could attain the highest levels of intellectual exploration. I've learned a lot working side-by-side with Director, and I feel like you've all learned much, too.

"Daddy, for instance, is learning that his consciousness is not merely connected to his physical body. His consciousness can survive being pancaked and liquefied and stuffed into a Ziploc bag. Mommy is learning that she can love a plastic doll as much as she can the mother that left her in a Target clothes rack. Linguiça is learning to see the world as a never-ending film. And Bloodman, well, he's learning that humanity can contain a demon in a small box.

"Tonight Director rests in a small box, too. We will end this memorial by closing the casket on Director's old life, and with him, we bury our old selves. Our old desires. Our selfish bodies leashed by an ego-driven consciousness. We can burn it all together. And we can finish this movie by getting to the top and confronting God or whatever the Hell sits atop that mountain."

Everyone cheered. They had energy anew. Mommy forgot about Baby's giant mass-produced body laying dead somewhere else on the mountain. Daddy forgot that his biggest asset was now just some fleshy goo in a Ziploc bag. Linguiça forgot that his body was almost completely overtaken by skin tags and tumors.

"Let's finish this fucking movie, epa!" They stood up and cheered as Translator slammed the casket closed and kicked it off its pedestal. Director came rolling out, dressed in a fitted tux and cowboy boots.

"May I present to you the birth of our new king!" Translator bowed.

Director stood up and dusted himself off.

"Hello, I am Director and we're going to finish this movie and make sense of it later! To understand your own creation is to lie to yourself, and we will never lie to ourselves or anyone else again. We will just present truth! The kind of truth that can be interpreted and shaped and misunderstood and devoured and digested and flushed down into the toilet of our minds to be forever forgotten. We are not ourselves when we aspire to be things we cannot be."

Spontaneously, they sang "Happy Birthday" to Director, and Director nodded at every line. He was well pleased with his little funeral. "Are you rolling?" he asked Linguiça.

"Baby, I'm always rolling. I think my brain keeps the battery charged now."

"You are the battery of human achievement, my friend. I love you sincerely. Translator, please hose this disgusting shit off our stars. By next week, the whole world will know their names!"

Translator pulled out a garden hose and cleaned them. The blood, mud, and cum fell from them like snakes shedding their skin to accommodate new growth. They were baptized into new people. Followers of Director forever.

CHPTR TN

TRANSLATOR PASSED THEM new scripts for the day. They were easier to read. There was no vowel guesswork.

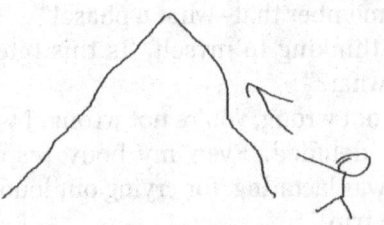

It was easy. Keep going up the mountain.

"Where's my lines?" Daddy was not offended. He was curious.

"Just a quick edit, one second." Director furrowed his brow and made a few adjustments.

"That's brilliant," Daddy said. "This is the role of a lifetime. Thank you, Director."

"Don't thank me. Thank yourselves. We are collaborating on my singular vision."

So they trudged up the mountain with a whole new gait of happiness and contentment. The scenery was no less blank, but things smelled better the closer they got to the top. Soft acoustic guitar and harpsichord was the cosmic soundtrack to their trek. They laughed and had moments of levity.

"Remember when you were all like, 'Where's my baby? Where's my baby?'" Linguiça chewed on his piece of bread like it was gum.

"I do remember that—what a phase!"

"I kept thinking to myself, 'Is this bitch completely deluded or what?'"

"You're not wrong, you're not wrong. I was completely and utterly deluded. Even my body responded to my delusion! I was lactating, for crying out loud!"

"What a trip."

Daddy laughed loud enough to try and wriggle himself into the conversation but nobody heard. A Ziploc bag does a pretty good job of muffling the sounds of social desperation. Try putting one over your head someday. People will think you're pathetic.

"Linguiça," Mommy said, "I think you're beautiful even though you're covered in skin problems."

"Thanks," Linguiça said. "Maybe you can help me tie these off when all is said and done here."

Translator passed another page of the script to them.

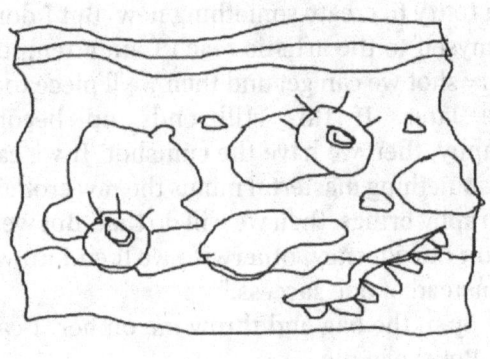

"Wow!" Daddy would've cried if he could. "A fucking monologue!"

Director smiled to see his first Apostle beaming with pride at the importance of his character. "You were the first converted believer. I lost a bet with Translator over this. I thought for sure you were going to be hot shit because of your extensive resume. Translator asked me if I thought you could deliver such a beautiful monologue considering you had the audacity to write in a no cumshot policy. But I said to him, I said, 'Listen, if a man believes in his own dick that fucking much that he doesn't even have to ejaculate to make his presence felt, then he will deliver his monologue beautifully.' You're just going to have to speak up and project because nobody can hear you from inside that bag."

"Anything for you, Director."

"We can have Linguiça stand in for the cumshot anyways."

Silence descended.

"What do you mean Linguiça is going to stand in for the cumshot?"

"As I slumbered in my coffin, I came to the realization

that I was thinking too highly of myself. My ego drove my ambition to try to create something new. But I don't want to limit myself to the artistic reach I am attempting. We need every shot we can get and then we'll piece together a narrative later. If this still ends up becoming a pornography, then we have the cumshot. If we can piece together something masterful minus the raw eroticism that a pornography brings, then we will do that. But we need to do both on our journey, otherwise we'll end up with two failures instead of one success."

"Just open the bag and throw me on her. I can do it, Director. Believe in me."

"I believe in you, but I will not believe in you enough to kill you. I will not believe in you enough to dishonor your contract."

If only I could open this bag up and kill myself, Daddy thought. His ego death was untrue. His ego had simply grown enough to trick himself into believing in the common cause of collaborative art.

All this time, ブラッドマン was a silent observer. No longer. "Director, you think you have killed their egos. You think that you have mindless robots to carry out your will, but you forget that I coated them with my blood and infected them forever."

Linguiça felt sick. "I can't chew bread anymore. It's like I'm not even Portuguese." He tumped over and contorted himself into ungodly shapes on the ground. His clean naked body was now dirtier than before ego death. Pain shot through every inch of his body. All of his skin tags fell off at once. There went first date plans with Mommy. Tiny geysers of blood shot out of wounds left by the dried-up skin tags.

Mommy, too. She fell to the floor in pain. She screamed when she suddenly realized, again, Baby was dead forever.

"You will have new children," ブラッドマン said. "The pain you are experiencing is the pain of childbirth. My blood coated your every pore just as the cumstorm happened. It was prophesied that I would finally bear fruit." Mommy and Linguiça's stomachs grew as if they were filled with little blood babies. (They were.) "You will never get to the top, Director. My army is gestating!"

"They can work through pregnancy," Translator said. His own silence made him uncomfortable. It felt good to break air again.

"How noble." ブラッドマン laughed. "Continue with your little film. You'll never finish it. You will all die before you reach the top."

"I hope I do!" Daddy whined like a teenager, but nobody listened because he couldn't project without a diaphragm.

CHPTR LVN

DIRECTOR RETREATED BACK to the cave he died in. "They do not listen to me," he said to himself over and over again. "They do not listen to me, and now they are pregnant. As soon as the pains of fetal development set in, they will forget about my art. They won't care. They'll have better things to do than participate in my vision."

"Can I help you with anything?" Translator needed to be necessary, and since Director's funeral, he felt himself to be a second dick. Nice to have in theory, but complicated to work with in practice.

"We either need to kill Bloodman, or we need to undo everything we did at the funeral."

"I have an idea. Stay in the cave today. I'll print some memorial t-shirts to remind them of your sacrifices and to cover their hideous naked bodies."

"I like it. There's a screen printer somewhere in this cave."

"I know where it is. I meant to get the shirts printed in time for the funeral but things started to move quickly. Felt like an unnecessary flourish. Turns out it was vital, and skipping it was a deadly mistake."

"Should I do the Italian stereotype again?" Director motioned around with his hands as he spoke.

"No. Please. Your hand motions don't match what you're saying at all."

"I've seen Italians in the wild. They flail around. It's disturbing."

"Get in the coffin. Play dead. This will work for some reason."

Director got into his coffin again, and as he laid down, he clutched at Translator's collar. "Translator, I am entrusting my everything to you. You are not my right hand man, you are not my left hand man. You are my hand man. Thank you for telling me to stop speaking with my hands."

"That's what I'm here for. Now close your eyes." As soon as Director closed his eyes, Translator shoved Director's face into the coffin and slammed it shut. Translator could hear the muffled screaming and confusion and pounding coming from inside. Translator pulled out a hammer and nails and nailed the coffin shut. He could hear the screaming fade into whimpers. "You will be immortal in death." Translator threw gasoline on the coffin and all around the cave, then he lit a cigarette and dropped it. The place went up in flames. As Translator walked out, he noticed Linguiça at the entrance of the cave. Linguiça just needed to pee in privacy. He didn't want to see this. Worse, he didn't want to have it on tape. He tried to pretend he was filming his feet, but it was no use. "What did you see?"

Linguiça answered, "Everything. I saw the part where you discussed pretending to be Italian again. I saw when you talked about t-shirts. And then I saw you shoving his head into the coffin, nailing it shut, and burning him alive."

"He was dead before I burned him alive." Realizing what he said, Translator said, "Fuck."

"At least it's on tape. We can cut it into something beautiful," Linguiça said. "I just have to pee. Ever since I found out I was pregnant, I have to pee all the time."

"Don't tell anyone what you saw here. This is

important. Even though Director died begging not to die, this is exactly what he would have wanted if only he would see things my way."

"Okay," Linguiça said, "I started peeing. I couldn't hold it anymore. You still going to make those shirts?"

"I made them already. Truth is, they were made in time for the funeral, but I got self-conscious and thought that maybe they were a bad idea, so I didn't bother."

"Can I see one?"

"What size are you?"

"Can you believe I used to be able to fit into a medium? Now I fluctuate between XL and XXL depending on the shirt. I'm sure it'll get worse with the bump."

Translator threw him a shirt. "See if it fits."

Nothing fit Linguiça normal anymore. "Don't make fun of me, but I have to put shirts on legs first now because of this thing." Linguiça pointed at the gangrenous camera. He threw his shirt on the ground and then put his feet through the collar. He pulled the shirt up as he wriggled side to side to fit the collar past his waist without stretching the elastic too much. Then he put one arm in at a time. The shirt fit well. Linguiça looked at the tag. XXL. Must be American made.

The t-shirt design was simple. A high-contrast black and white image of Director was on the chest with the words, *"Some people never really live . . . Some people never really die . . . "* The joke was funnier when the whole plan was to fake Director's death. Director was dead for sure now. No wooden coffin would survive that hellfire. And even if he did, the coffin was nailed shut.

"Let's put out this fire and check the coffin to make sure he's dead." Translator was a worrier.

"Keep the fire going if you want to be sure."

ブラッドマン's box floated in behind Linguiça. "Do not

worry so much." A devious smile snuck across ブラッドマン's face. There was something about ブラッドマン's eyes. They floated in their net of blood vessels and never seemed uncalm. It was disarming. It could be hypnotizing.

"I will not worry," Translator said. He clapped his hands and said, "Okay, Linguiça. Let's go to the top of that mountain!" Translator's assuredness quickly turned sour. He grabbed Linguiça by his brand-new shirt and shoved their faces together. "And don't you tell a fucking soul what you saw here. That's for the editing room floor, you worthless sausage."

"Okay."

ブラッドマン's floating box led the procession out of the cave. Hovering above them in the blank nothingness of space, TV screens had wings. They were flying in place, and they were tuned to what looked like hostage interviews under duress. They weren't just any hostages. They were watching themselves. There was familiarity behind the cacophony of distressed voices describing something inaudibly. Their words did not seem sincere even though nobody could hear exactly what they were saying. Each of them looked just off camera at some unknown person for directions. They nodded. This unknown person must have had a gun or something because every time they nodded, they also flinched like they were about to meet the butt-end of a gun. It wasn't clear if what was playing was a continuous shot or a very smooth loop, but Translator was immediately unsettled.

"When did you film these?" He shook Linguiça by the shoulders.

Linguiça pointed to the TVs. He was on now. There was no camera fleshed onto his face, but there was a giant hole where that part of his face was. On TV, he pointed to it almost as if it was a nervous tic. "I wish they'd turn on captions," he said, "I wish I knew what I was saying."

"When did you sit down for an interview?"

"Don't you get it?" Linguiça was impatient. "There's some kind of time warp going on. Maybe we're stuck just outside the loop. Maybe we're on this fucking mountain forever."

"You don't know anything about spacetime. I am a prodigious reader. I've read about time loops and dimensional destruction and multiversal traversal and decay. I've never read anything close to what we're going through."

Mommy ran up to them as they argued. "Something is wrong with Daddy." She held up the Ziploc bag. His gelatinous and near-liquid parts congealed into a single block. His eyes were yellow and his teeth had fallen out of the gums they were held to.

"He just needs water," ブラッドマン said. "Maybe just some pee. The same thing that brought me back to life. Consciousness is a funny thing, isn't it?"

"I . . . want . . . I want . . . to die . . . "

"He wants to die!" Mommy did not know how to feel about this. On one hand, he was a burden to carry around. On the other hand, she had said many times in her life that she wanted to die but probably would have regretted dying had she got her wish. A fleeting moment of despair was worthy of suffering through to get to healing. She heard that in a talking Hallmark card once. But the writer probably didn't inhabit a Ziploc bag.

"Just . . . empty me . . . onto the ground."

"Ashes to ashes and dust to dust," ブラッドマン laughed. "I would give him what he desires."

It was Daddy's turn on the big screen. He had a body and a smile. He didn't seem held against his will. All of the TVs were now tuned to him and the words were easier to make out.

"Oh, yeah. It was a great opportunity for me to be in one of Director's films. I was a fan of his vision from the start. No more *t* and *h* together, drop vowels, throw in some hieroglyphics. I mean, it was wild and important stuff up on that mountain. Without his, uh . . . let's just admit it was absolutely insane, without his vision . . . I wouldn't be here talking to you. I probably would have put a bag over my head and killed myself at work a long, long time ago. Sometimes existence is meaningless. Sometimes meaninglessness is existence. Director taught me the lies that got me to the truth. I have purpose now."

The unknown body behind the camera pulled out a gun and pointed it at Daddy.

"I am not afraid. You are filming. This is art. In death, I become immortal because I participated." Daddy smiled and looked directly at the camera. His eyes were vacant, but he continued his speech. "The residue of my existence will permeate all things. While the knowledge of my existence may diminish with time and memory, my influence is long lasting. I have no fears." He stared directly into the camera, and the cameraman must have been to art school because he slowly zoomed in on the eyes until he could not. There was no discovery in the zoom. The eyes were empty and hollow. His gaze must have haunted them.

"That's nice," the cameraman said and pulled the trigger. The TVs floated away and the atmosphere returned to the empty void.

"Please . . . kill me . . . " It's like Daddy didn't even watch his amazing, life-affirming speech in the face of his murder.

"Daddy," Mommy brought the bag right up to her face. "What if that was you in the future? You might be able to recover from this long enough to find happiness and then be murdered on tape."

"If . . . I could puncture . . . this bag . . . I would . . . that's why . . . all my teeth are . . . floating . . . I willed them out . . . of their sockets . . . in the false hope . . . they'd puncture . . . the bag . . . kill me . . . please."

"Hey, has anyone noticed Linguiça's new shirt?" Translator was impatient with how quickly his plans were distracted by others' emotional needs.

"I . . . don't care . . . "

"Director is dead?" Mommy put her hand to her mouth.

"Very dead. He asked me to give him a viking's funeral. So I burned him in his casket. There are no rivers up here, as you can see, so I had to leave him in his cave. But he's dead. Do you want to see him?"

"Let the dead bury the dead," ブラッドマン said.

"That's great, who said that?" Linguiça asked.

"It is cosmic knowledge. It is demonic intellect. It is angelic happenstance."

ブラッドマン laughed from the bottom of where his belly would be. It was deep and microtonal. It shook the mountain. It caused the universe around them to burst with light for a moment and then go completely dark. "Power surge," ブラッドマン said. "Rare but devastating. Only our desire can light the way."

Translator pulled out a few pages of script. "If anybody cares!" He waved his papers around. "We still need to finish Director's vision." Translator wrote his own text in the moments nobody paid attention to him. He worked so closely with Director that he felt he could ape his style with no telltale signs of forgery.

"Oh, I care," Mommy said. She grabbed her script.

MOTHER

Wherefore unbeknownst to myne breast,
henceforth blow forth thyne lactose
liquid for the furtherment of human
exploration and thee frontiers of
thyne own mind.

FATHER

Mine body cast within a plastic big
as if I were cursed to be an
amphibious rodent won as a prize at a
carnival for children.

MOTHER

Whatsoever hath God wrought upon myne
empty mind? Myne body is tired, Lord.
Wherefore whencefest may I go?

"Too many vowels," Mommy said.

"It was an early draft," Translator said.

"How early? . . . I haven't been . . . in this . . . incredibly durable Ziploc . . . bag the whole . . . time . . . "

"Before the vowels dropped and after the Ziploc bag. Ziploc sure makes a good product, don't they?" Translator tried to change the subject.

"I've never had any experience with any other kind of bag. I wouldn't know what to call it if not for Ziploc. That shows the trust I have in their product," Mommy said as she looked into Linguiça's camera face.

Linguiça gave her a thumbs up and then turned to ブラッドマン. "Your writing is terrible. False profundity put on by a verbosity that anyone with the intellect the size of a lizard's could spot as an insecurity from a mile away. You needed Director more than Director needed you."

But there was no time for a bitch fight between Translator and ブラッドマン. Linguiça was having contractions. He writhed on the floor.

Translator untied the laces from his shoes and tied them with slipknots around Linguiça's ankles. "We're getting to the fucking top. Fuck the script. We're getting to the top if we have to drag his ass the entire way." Translator tied the shoelaces to

ブラッドマン's floating box. ブラッドマン did not mind this responsibility. "And Linguiça! You better keep filming!"

Linguiça whispered to Mommy, "He acts like I can turn this fucking thing off. Director told me I was the battery to the world or something. I wish I could turn it off. I wish it would fall off my fucking face already. I'm with child, and I got this fucking thing completely absorbed into my body."

"I'm starting to feel kicks," Mommy said. "But they are kicking toward my back rather than my belly and it feels sharp. Not like baby feet at all. I don't know, I have nothing to compare to. I've never been pregnant."

"Neither have I," Linguiça said. "It hurts like hell. I feel more empathy for my own mom when she used to beat me with a broom. This is torture. Augghhhhhh!" He screamed as ブラッドマン started to pull away. Mommy clutched Daddy in her palm and followed in a slow trot. She was bowlegged. Whatever was in her was about to fall out. She felt it climb her body from the inside, tearing at every internal organ as it passed it. Her gag reflex kicked in. She dry heaved. Translator screamed, "If we have to stop every time you are in existential terror, we will never finish this fucking thing!"

Mommy opened her mouth. Two hooves climbed out, stretching her lips until they looked like used balloons. Her jaw separated. A hoofed, human child fell out and screamed. Mommy rushed to the floor and wiped the phlegm and yellow crusty vernix off the baby. When it was rubbed off, Mommy could see that its skin was transparent and visible to all who cared were the inner workings of a body. You could even see the lightning-strike synapses of its still-smooth brain. "You are beautiful," Mommy said. Mommy sat with her freak child and stuck her nipple in its mouth. It refused. "You ungrateful little shit."

ブラッドマン laughed. "Its genetic makeup is mostly pulled from shit from every creature on earth. It *is* a little shit."

"Nobody asked you," Mommy said.

"Let's keep moving," Translator said. "Linguiça wants to get back home. This job has gotten old to him."

"I'm fucking dying, man. I could do this all day, but I gotta get my face checked out by a professional."

"You look fine," Translator said. But Linguiça was on the ground with his ass up as tentacles squirmed their way out of his anus. He screamed bloody murder. But the child was the spitting image of Linguiça; the head, at least. He had no body, he was all tentacle. Director benefited from mystique. Translator had no mystery. He was just an egghead who knew too much, and he believed that blessed him with the ability to govern. It did not. It rarely does. He carried a gun, and I'm sorry I didn't mention it before, but even I didn't know he did. He shot it in the air. Quiet descended real quick. That's how you get what you want. You wave a gun around. If you aren't that skilled with people, you oughta try violence. Especially if you want your way.

"Listen, you fuckers. Shut the hell up. Director is dead and I'm taking over. We're going up. We only have a little way to go."

ブラッドマン moved forward again. He said nothing. He did not want to further upset Translator. It wasn't worth the risk. Translator's body would be his to inhabit as soon as they reached the top of the mountain. ブラッドマン needed just one more cumstorm and a lightning strike, and he would be free of his box. The last good body left was Translator's. Upsetting him too much might cause him to kill himself. People like Linguiça never have the good sense to try. Translator was smart enough to know at a certain point, it wasn't worth going any further with this whole thing we call consciousness.

Linguiça held his octopus baby as he was dragged across the dried and dusty trail by ブラッドマン. He couldn't help but love this weird thing. His face and facial expressions were very much genetic; he smiled like Linguiça, he already had a unibrow, and he was easy to make laugh. A face is one thing; a mind is another. Was he more octopus than man? His avô ate octopus soup often. Slurped it up with a glass of port wine. It smelled like carcass to Linguiça, but his avô liking it was enough to get Linguiça to try it. Linguiça smiled at the memory he forgot he had. It had been so long since he smelled anything but shit that he forgot how comforting his avô's cologne of red wine and cigarette smoke was. Avô quit smoking with a plastic cigarette, but nobody ever quits smoking. In the backyard, Linguiça twisted his ankle in a hole filled with half-smoked cigarettes. He hid it from everyone. Another's mind is another planet. Unreachable. He loved avô, and he loved his weirdo freak octopus son that looked exactly like him. For the first time, Linguiça forgot he had a camera melded into his face.

The more Mommy looked at her hoofed child, the more disgusted she was by it. Its transparent skin was unearthly, almost industrial. The kid may have been a robot. He came out looking sixteen years old at three feet tall. She dry heaved as she held its hoof.

"Bipedal, even," ブラッドマン said.

"Yeah." Mommy shrugged. "He seems more high maintenance than Baby, if I'm being honest."

At the top of the mountain was a door. ブラッドマン pointed to it. "There is the end of our journey and the beginning of what comes next."

"A door?" Mommy was confused. "We hoofed it—no offense—" she pointed to her kid, "—all the way up this fucking mountain to see a wooden door, connected to nothing but the deep void of space? What's behind that door? Gee, I wonder!" Mommy was pissed. She made overly theatrical hand movements like she might have some Italian in her genes. She mimed opening a door and looking through it. "Oh, look everybody! It's more fucking nothing! It's more emptiness! It's more vacuum! It's more confusion! It's more futility! I want off this fucking mountain." She got down to her knees and prayed to the heavens which, by most terrestrial accounts, she was already within. "Please get me off this mountain."

They floated off the ground. All of them. Including ブラッドマン. His supernatural trickery was no match for the lack of gravity. It was gradual, so no one noticed it until they looked around and saw the others.

"We must reach that door, or the prophecy will not be fulfilled, and we will all perish." It was the first time ブラッドマン sounded worried.

"Boo-fucking-hoo," Translator said, but he didn't add anything else. He was just being a wet blanket, as usual. He needed Director to balance out his weaknesses. Without Director, he was just a guy nobody wanted to be around.

Linguiça felt queasy. "Is the mountain spinning, or is the universe spinning?"

They looked around. The stars were streaking around them. All of everything was spinning.

"I think we're the center of the universe right now," Daddy said. The humidity of his breath fogged up the Ziploc bag. "I think that's me." Daddy was right. His body was floating lifeless, naked, and emaciated. His eyelids open, eyes wide, looking euphoric towards his Ziploc bag. The body's mouth didn't move but everyone heard him say, "Ah, you have transcended body for a superior Ziploc bag. I am proud of you."

Soon, they'd recognize all of their bodies floating lifeless in the nothingness of space. No other spoke to them, though, as only Daddy had truly left his body to become goo.

ブラッドマン was impatient. "We need to stop this spinning. We need to get to the door."

Translator, in a high-pitched, mocking tone answered right back, "We need to stop this spinning. We need to get to the door." He dropped a few octaves and then said, "Shut the fuck up. You need to find your body."

ブラッドマン could not remember his form prior to becoming ブラッドマン.

"I have been a cosmic sojourner for so long that I am empty of all memories of my prior form." He felt sadness—something he hadn't felt in ages. He felt emptiness. He felt something about how everything seemed to amount to nothing and that sure seemed like something. Yellow butterflies swirled around them.

"I am the butterfly." The spinning slowed down. The roadkill corpses of deformed animals arose and danced a morbid number, strung up as corpse puppets.

"I am the nuke dogs of Chernobyl." The spinning slowed even more. Cum, sweat, blood, tears, farts, poop, smiles, hatred, queef dust, love all took physical forms above them. ブラッドマン laughed. He laughed maniacally.

"I am God." The spinning stopped. Gravity restored their asses back to the ground. "We must open that door."

When they opened that door, they were in a barren, wood-paneled office. There was a desk in the middle. There was a portrait of the President of the United States behind the desk. Behind the desk was the charred body of Director. He was lifeless, but Translator did a great job embalming; skin melting off his skeleton looked like dried candle wax. His face was frozen in a scream. His body smelled like burnt pepperoni and Campari. It could have been nobody but Director.

The lights in the office flickered on and off.

At the front of the desk was a name placard that read, "God."

Without any warning, Director's candle wax body burst into flames and he fell into laughter. He stood up.

"Let me show you my buttons," he said. At his desk was a mixing board filled with thousands of buttons but only one was labeled. It was somewhere in the middle, and there was a Post It note pasted to it that said, "Cumstorm." Director's skeleton pressed the button over and over and over again. He screamed with laughter.

Thunder, lightning, and creampie rain. The ceiling drooped as the cum overburdened its supports. Soon the room would be full of cum, and they'd all die.

"Translator, you have betrayed me," Flaming Skeleton Director said. His skin dripped onto the floor and spattered into tiny replicas of Director down to the cum mustache. Ziploc Bag Daddy was able to shift his weight enough from one end of the bag to the other to free himself from Mommy's grip. He fell to the floor and almost unzipped but luck was on his side.

"Director, you have returned!" Daddy screamed as loud as he could, but there was a lot going on, and everybody had gotten used to ignoring him so nobody heard him. Not even Director. ブラッドマン was blinking morse code to Translator. Translator nodded in complete agreement as he saw Director march toward him, metaphorically burning with murderous passion and, also, burning burning.

"You betrayed me."

Linguiça was upright. It was the first time in a while. He smiled and chewed bubblegum while showing his kid the ropes. With eight tentacles, the boy could really give him a hand. The boy held up the camera for Linguiça to relieve the pressure and constant bleeding. It was great. Linguiça really took to raising a creature like few alcoholics can. "This is going to be a fucking masterpiece."

Translator ran to Mommy. "I need your kid."

"Sure," Mommy said. "Hey, Hoof Hands! Go with the nice man." Hoof Hands agreed and bleated his approval.

Translator got on his knees and made some hand gestures against the box

ブラッドマン was trapped inside. Hoof Hands nodded and used its hooves to beat against the box until it broke. When it shattered, ブラッドマン spilled out and formed himself back into the shape of a man made of pulsating blood vessels, constantly pumping and forever leaking. Translator ran to Daddy and unzipped the Ziploc. By this time, all that remained of Director's flesh had melted into smaller Directors running around doing nothing but irritating people the way fleas do. Ultimately killable if you have the patience to swat endlessly. Translator threw Daddy's liquified mix onto Director's skeleton. Immediately, the flesh began to thread around the bones. He didn't look exactly like Daddy, but he looked close enough.

The ceiling cracked with more thunder, and buckets of

giant fish-sized sperm filled the room, frantic and looking for giant eggs to fuck up forever. ブラッドマン grabbed one out of thin air, opened his wind-up mouth, and swallowed it whole. He grabbed at Director Daddy, unhinged his jaw, and swallowed him whole. "Now, I am become Death. Destroyer of worlds." ブ ラ ッ ド マ ン laughed.

"Cheesy and cliche," Mommy said. Hoof Hands looked to Mommy for approval, but she couldn't care less about whatever the fuck it was doing anymore. "Go play with the demon."

Hoof Hands nodded and clomped over to ブラッドマーン. ブ ラッ ドマン grabbed Hoof Hands and consumed him whole, too. But Hoof Hands's hands were too hoofy and kicked free of ブラッドマン's blood body. Hoof Hands scurried away to the comfort of Mommy whose elation turned to resigned depression as Hoof Hands rubbed his head at her legs for reassurance. She pet his head and wiped her hands clean. The tears in ブ ラ ッ ド マ ン's pumping vessels healed themselves and ブラッドマン grew angry. Soon, ブラッドマン was eating every physical object in his sight. He was a black hole and the world was ending. A blood and cum tornado touched down inside the office swirling everything into ブラッドマン's orbit. "Ha! Ha! Ha! Translator!"

Translator pissed himself. "Yes?"

"You destroy meaning." ブラッドマン grabbed him by the eyes, lifted him up, and bit Translator's head off.

Linguiça was vibing. He bobbed his head at the great shots his octopus kid was able to intuit. "Hell yeah, this runs in the family!" The octopus freak slid his tentacle underneath where the flesh and camera met and accidentally hit REC. He didn't know any better. Couldn't blame the kid. But as soon as that button was pressed, the cum dried up, the tornado dissipated, and ブラッドマン became a pile of dried scabs. Translator was still dead. Director's charred skeleton was lifeless. But there was a Ziploc bag that Daddy's pile of goo was able to move back inside. "I'm alive," he said. "I'm fucking alive."

"We'll find some way to get a body back on you, bud," Linguiça said.

Linguiça opened the door and stepped out onto the mountain. Hoof Hands, Tentacles, Daddy, and Mommy followed. The door splintered away after they closed it.

"Remember when we were kids?" Linguiça held his octopus son's tentacle tight. "We used to roll down hills. Just throw our fate to gravity? Let's do that."

Mommy went to Hoof Hands. "I don't want you to roll. It's too dangerous. You stay here, let Mommy make sure it's safe." Hoof Hands bleated nervousness but nodded. Mommy held onto Daddy in his Ziploc bag. "We'll finally be out of this mess," she whispered. One by one, they rolled all the way down the mountain back to Earth.

"It was nice meeting y'all." Linguiça stuck out his hand. "I'll look at the footage I have after I get this camera surgically removed and see what we can do about it. I think it's actually going to be good."

Mommy shook Linguiça's hand. "Yeah, I had a great time. Have fun with your kid. You two seem to really be great together."

"Don't really have a choice," Linguiça laughed. "Just gotta make the best of it."

"Uh huh." Mommy looked at the baggy Daddy was in and realized he must have leaked out during all that rolling.

"Where's Hoofy?" Linguiça asked.

"Who?" Mommy did the best acting she had ever done in her life with that one word.

"Daddy okay?"

"Yeah, I stuffed him up my ass because I figured that was safest while rolling." It was a good lie. A good plan, too. It's too bad she thought of it too late.

The End

THE SCRIPT IN FRAGMENTS WITH NO EXPLANATIONS BUT VOWELS HAVE BEEN RESTORED FOR CLARITY

I. - IE - OI

OY a e io a a. e aea ao oe a e iooi.
e i iaie; e a e y e aua oee. ou i e
ae i e e? a e oo iaie o a oee? ou i
ieiay u ay a ooy ou ie e ayay?

AY ie io a ou a ea e ae. e oe.

OY
I e ie u.

AY
I e ie ooy u u.

AY e ou o i ai, ou e ii o e ie o i ae
yoii i aeou aia-ie aue, a a OY y e i.

AY (O')
e e o ooy u u a iee y ai. I ao oo ye.

OY' eye ie, ui i aio, yoii e aeou
aia-ie aue.

OY
I u a o a a u ui oo oe ou o y uoe.

e oo I oy ei IEO. e a ee e ieiy o i o
a e o a a o i ea oe o i ei. e ea. i e
ee. e, u a e aea e a oe a i a iou oui
ieo, ieo oo oe i oue, eye ie aiy io e
aea' e.

IEO
ae-a you a! e a ii i-a oe ou!

AE O A A E EE O O UAAI AE I

IE A:

OY
I ou ae o ee oe i oy I a o e ee ai e
e o a a-o-ye uioee ouai i e ie o e
iy.

AY
I' o eey ay oe aea.

OY
I oe o ay eoe ae ea.

AY
[ay, aia eye, ea]
e'e aie. e'e aie a a' a a ae.

e a o AY ii o e oo, oee i u.

OY
I oe i.

AY
e i e e a o a e oiey.

OY
o i I o i?

AY
e i e e ouaio y u i ui uo.

OY
I oo aou i.

AY:
u u. e i e a ai i.

OY:
I i' o I oe i.

OY (O')
Þ a ai ou aÞ.

AY
o i Þ i?

OY
Þ i ee eaeuy, auay Þouou ou ouey.

e a o o, eye oe, eei eaeuy a auay.

AY
Þa ae e ay. oo!

ay oi o e a.

AY (O')
Þ oea ai ou ay.

OY
aie.

oy o i. a o e ee. ea i oo yi ou o e
ouÞ.

ue & ie, OY a AY o e e a ie oe a oe
aai. AY i i ey ai u oe eoie o e oe Þa
i a ee ee eoe.

OY (O')
I o o o i I a oiue.

AY
oee. e ae Þi ouey u Þ ouai & e i ii
i.

OY
a i Þ ouey' oi ayoe? e ae a i. Þ i u
e oee.

AY
aee i ao Þa ouai, e i ui i & e i i ou
& i i ie u ie e ou ee iaie.

OY:
o i ao Þa ouai.

AY:
Þe e i i i, e, Þe, Þa, i.

AY oo u & i i ie.

AY (O')
e'e ee a Þi o o Þa y a i.

OY
I' o oeÞi I' oee iÞ.

OY ue AY ie. AY uea.

Þy u ua. oy ay ay o e a. ay i oi.

OY (O')
ao o youe.

AY
I' oa y Þ a Þi o ou y.

OY a ay aou iÞ ea.

OY
a' e oi oe iÞ Þi i aou.

OY o.

AY
e a o o ae aa. y oa u.

OY
ay ee ee. ay ee i. aa a ai.

AY
You oay ey Þ ee o y e. eÞe i e aa,
aa, o ea.

OY
Þee i oeÞi ie Þa u oi o ee. eae o' Þi
I a o oeeae o you ee. I a u uoee ou o
ioiy. I oe you.

AY:
You ae oe. I a o oe ye. I a e.

o ae e i a ooy ou ay o i ay e i ou o.

OY i ay oe e ea iy, eye oi ou, aeu eae.

OY
I a oi o i e oi a e e o e uiee a I a
oi o e i.

OY (O')
ay ea. e u ea. e u o io iee.

AY
I ae o a. I ae o e. u a. I' uee.

OY
I' y uy o ae ae o i ye. I ou ay i. o
I u oue i.

OY a o. ae o o ou. ea, oo, ae. ou. ea
ie.

XCRMNTMNTN

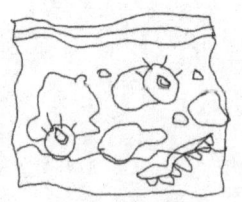

OE
eeoe ueo o ye ea, eeo o o ye aoe iui
o e uee o ua eoaio a ee oie o ye o i.

AE
ie oy a ii a ai i a i I ee ue o e a
aiiou oe o a a ie a a aia o ie.

OE
aoee a o ou uo ye ey i? ye oy i ie,
o. eeoe eee ay I o?

Acknowledgements

Nina, my wife, is always the first to hear a sentence or paragraph I'm working on. She is patient with me and sometimes will give me a laugh where none is deserved. She is loving and supportive and backed my decision to buy a bidet, increasing our home's value tenfold. My kids run around the house wild and free and make finding the brief moments of calm to write much more productive. They are beautiful and provide a whole new lens to see the world through. I'm lucky, too, because they really love poop jokes. My friends: Max, Miguel, Zach and Trey. They were the first to hear about XCRMNTMNTN which was formed in a lockdown-induced depression. I was embarrassed from having no creative output and was fueled by pure jealousy at their productivity. Colorado Cheryl and Santa Ana Jack: two friends and creative collaborators that I miss seeing all the time and I wish space didn't equal distance. My family far away in California, thank you for answering my calls and reminding me that I sound very crazy just by virtue of being in Texas. Max gets thanked twice because Max and Lori are wonderful people and great publishers and I am forever grateful for their friendship and our high-stakes, mega-profit business relationship. I think this is a good book and I hope you did, too.

ABOUT THE AUTHOR

Andrew Hilbert is the author of *Inner Space, Invasion of the Weirdos, Bangface & the Gloryhole,* and *Death Thing.* He lives in Texas.

SPOOKY TALES FROM GHOULISH BOOKS 2023

LIKE REAL | Shelly Lyons

ISBN: 978-1-943720-82-8 $16.95

This mind-bending body horror rom-com is a rollicking Cronenbergian gene splice of *Idle Hands* and *How to Lose a Guy in 10 Days*. It's freaky. It's fun. It's LIKE REAL.

XCRMNTMNTN | Andrew Hilbert

ISBN: 978-1-943720-81-1 $14.95

When a pile of shit from space lands near a renowned filmmaker's set, inspiration strikes. Take a journey up a cosmic mountain of excrement with the director and his film crew as they ascend into madness led only by their own vanity and obsession. This is a nightmare about creation. This is a dream about poop. This is a call to arms against vowels. This is *XCRMNTMNTN*.

BOUND IN FLESH | edited by Lor Gislason

ISBN: 978-1-943720-83-5 $16.95

Bound in Flesh: An Anthology of Trans Body Horror brings together 13 trans and non-binary writers, using horror to both explore the darkest depths of the genre and the boundaries of flesh. A disgusting good time for all! Featuring stories by Hailey Piper, Joe Koch, Bitter Karella, and others.

CONJURING THE WITCH | Jessica Leonard

ISBN: 978-1-943720-84-2 $16.95

Conjuring the Witch is a dark, haunted story about what those in power are willing to do to stay in power, and the sins we convince ourselves are forgivable.

WHAT HAPPENED WAS IMPOSSIBLE |
E. F. Schraeder

ISBN: 978-1-943720-85-9 $14.95

Everyone knows the woman who escapes a massacre is a final girl, but who is the final boy? *What Happened Was Impossible* follows the life of Ida Wright, a man who knows how to capitalize on his childhood tragedies . . . even when he caused them.

THE ONLY SAFE PLACE LEFT IS THE DARK|
Warren Wagner

ISBN: 978-1-943720-86-6 $14.95

In *The Only Safe Place Left is the Dark*, an HIV positive gay man must leave the relative safety of his cabin in the woods to brave the zombie apocalypse and find the medication he needs to stay alive.

THE SCREAMING CHILD| Scott Adlerberg

ISBN: 978-1-943720-87-3 $16.95

Scott Adlerberg's *The Screaming Child* is a mystery horror novel told by a grieving woman working on a book about an explorer who was murdered in a remote wilderness region, only to get caught up in a dangerous journey after hearing the distant screams from her own vanished child somewhere in the woods.

RAINBOW FILTH | Tim Meyer

ISBN: 978-1-943720-88-0 $14.95

Rainbow Filth is a weirdo horror novella about a small cult that believes a rare psychedelic substance can physically transport them to another universe.

LET THE WOODS KEEP OUR BODIES| E. M. Roy

ISBN: 978-1-943720-89-7 $16.95

The familiar becomes strange the longer you look at it. Leo Bates navigates a broken sense of reality, shattered memories, and a distrust of herself in order to find her girlfriend Tate and restore balance to their hometown of Eston—if such a thing ever existed to begin with.

SAINT GRIT| Kayli Scholz

ISBN: 978-1-943720-90-3 $14.95

One brooding summer, Nadine Boone pricks herself on a poisonous manchineel tree in the Florida backcountry. Upon self-orgasm, Nadine conjures a witch that she calls Saint Grit. Pitched as *Gummo* meets *The Craft*, Saint Grit grows inside of Nadine over three decades, wreaking repulsive havoc on a suspicious cast of characters in a small town known as Sugar Bends. Comes in Censored or Uncensored cover.

Ghoulish Books
PO Box 1104
Cibolo, TX 78108

☐ LIKE REAL   16.95

☐ XCRMNTMNTN   14.95

☐ BOUND IN FLESH   16.95

☐ CONJURING THE WITCH   16.95

☐ WHAT HAPPENED WAS IMPOSSIBLE   14.95

☐ THE ONLY SAFE PLACE LEFT IS THE DARK   14.95

☐ THE SCREAMING CHILD   16.95

☐ RAINBOW FILTH   14.95

☐ LET THE WOODS KEEP OUR BODIES   16.95

☐ SAINT GRIT   14.95
    Censored | Uncensored

Ship to:

Name _____

Address _____

City_____State_____Zip _____

Phone Number _____

                              Book Total: $_____

                          Shipping Total: $_____

                            Grand Total: $_____

Not all titles available for immediate shipping. All credit card
purchases must be made online at GhoulishBooks.com. Shipping is
5.80 for one book and an additional dollar for each additional book.
Contact us for international shipping prices. All checks and money
orders should be made payable to Perpetual Motion Machine.

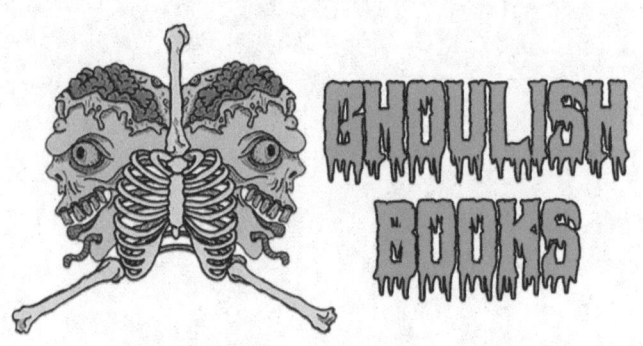

Patreon:
www.patreon.com/pmmpublishing

Website:
www.GhoulishBooks.com

Facebook:
www.facebook.com/GhoulishBooks

Twitter:
@GhoulishBooks

Instagram:
@GhoulishBookstore

Newsletter:
www.PMMPNews.com

Linktree:
linktr.ee/ghoulishbooks

www.ingramcontent.com/pod-product-compliance
Lightning Source LLC
Chambersburg PA
CBHW011518240626
47154CB00010B/3082